W9-AUI-721

Mighty Mighty **MONSTERS**

HIDE and SHRIEK!

STONE ARCH BOOKS
a capstone imprint

Mighty Mighty MONSTERS

HIDE and SHRIEK!

created by Sean O'Reilly
illustrated by Arcana Studio

Mighty Mighty Monsters are published by Stone Arch Books, A Capstone Imprint
151 Good Counsel Drive, P.O. Box 669 Mankato, Minnesota 56002 *www.capstonepub.com*

Library of Congress Cataloging-in-Publication Data
O'Reilly, Sean, 1974-
  Hide and shriek / written by Sean O'Reilly ; illustrated by Arcana Studio.
    p. cm. -- (Mighty Mighty Monsters)
  Summary: Before the Mighty Mighty Monsters can play hide-and-seek, they need to
make some rules such as no flying like a vampire bat, no sniffing like a werewolf, and no
using magic.
  ISBN 978-1-4342-2148-3 (library binding)
  1. Graphic novels. [1. Graphic novels. 2. Monsters--Fiction. 3. Hide-and-seek--Fiction.] I.
Arcana Studio. II. Title.
  PZ7.7.O74Hid 2010
  741.5'973--dc22   2010004122

Printed in the United States of America in Stevens Point, Wisconsin.
032010
005741WZF10

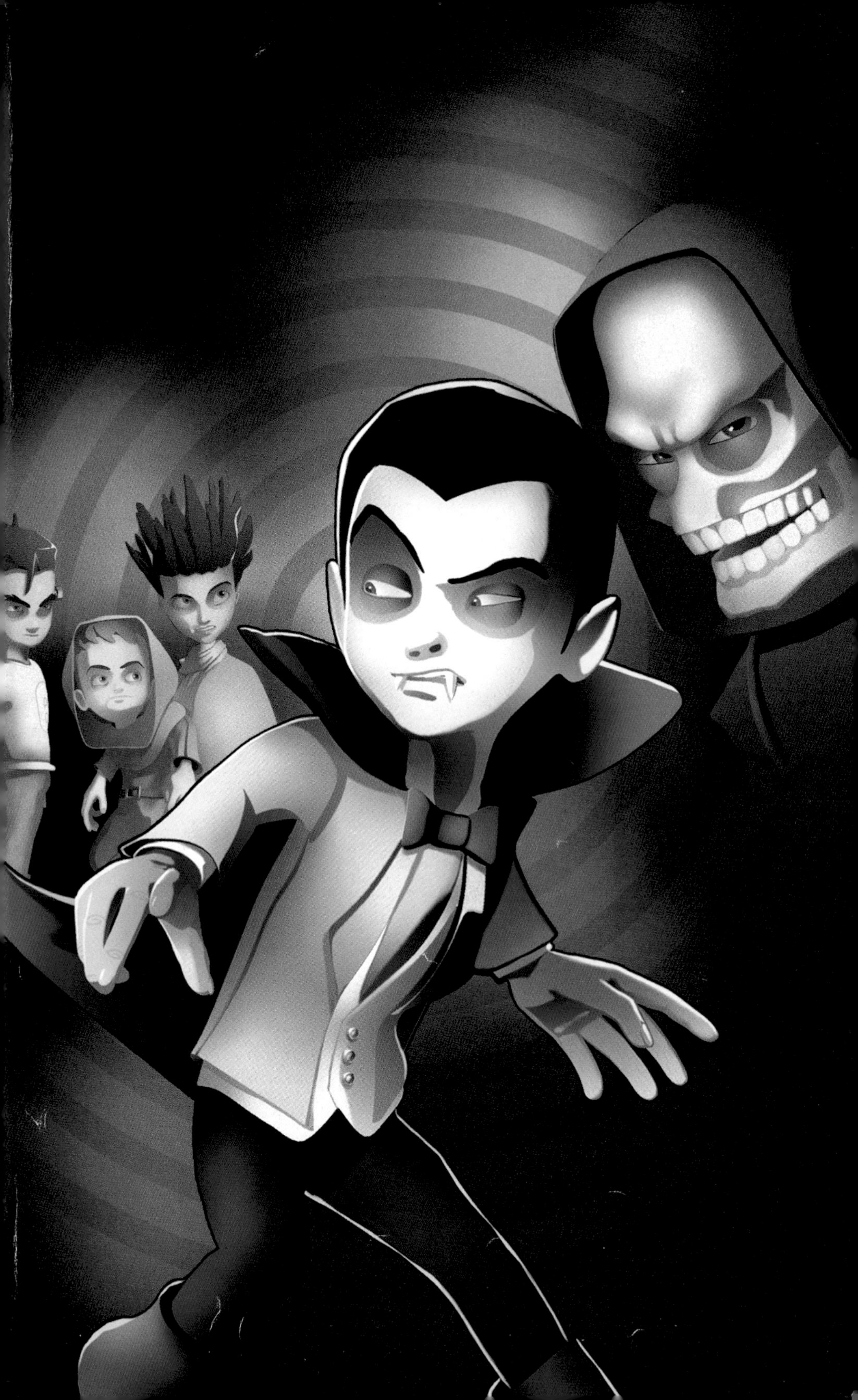

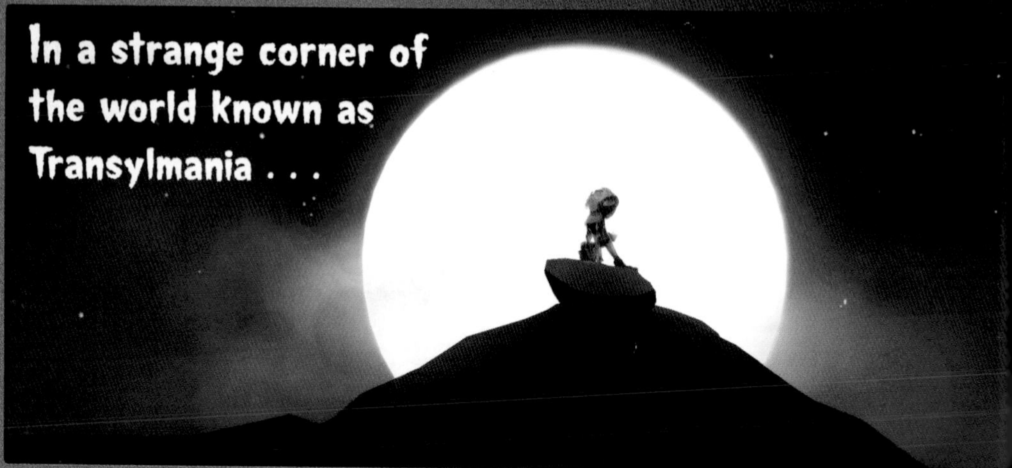
In a strange corner of the world known as Transylmania . . .

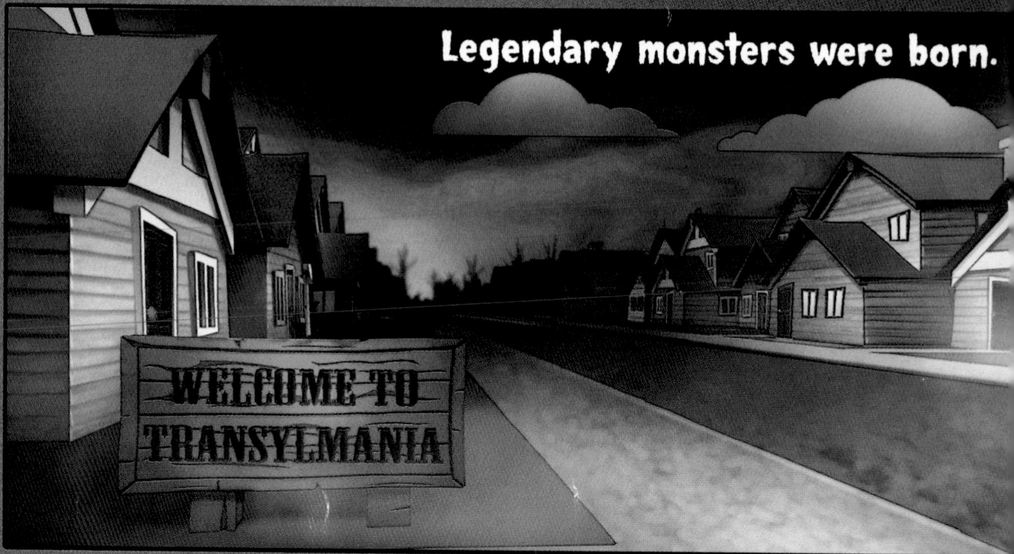
Legendary monsters were born.
WELCOME TO TRANSYLMANIA

But long before their frightful fame, these classic creatures faced fears of their own.

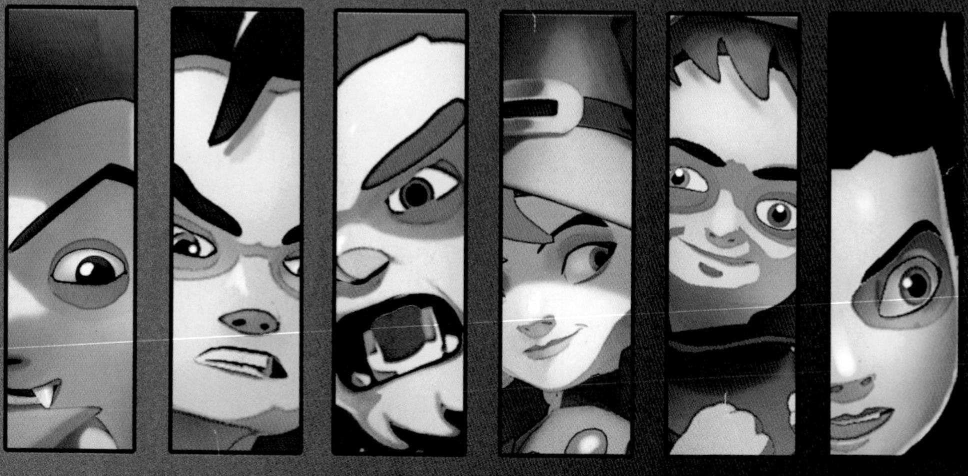

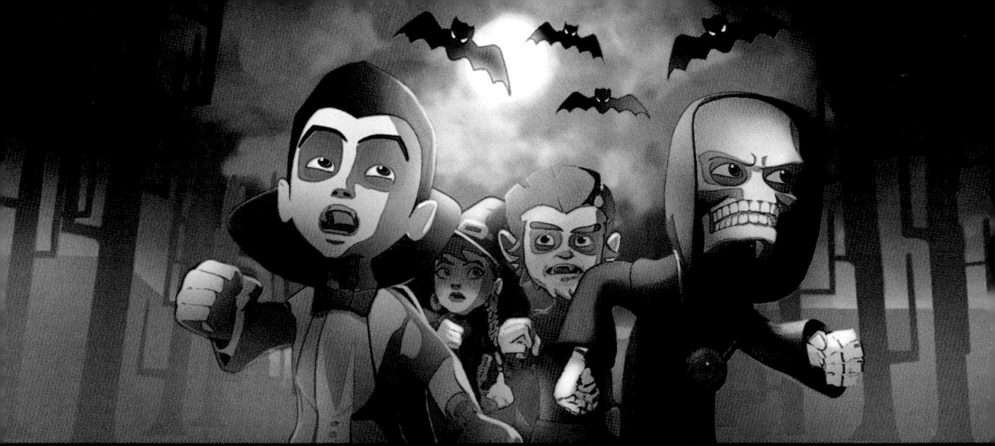

o take on terrifying teachers and homework horrors,
hey formed the most fearsome friendship on Earth . . .

Mighty Mighty MONSTERS

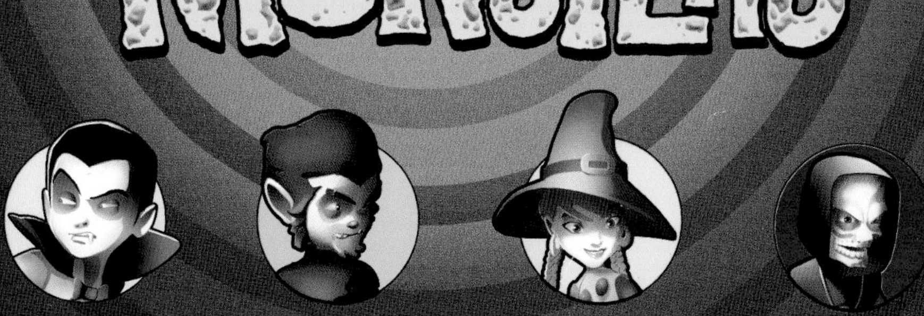

Vlad Talbot Witchita Milton

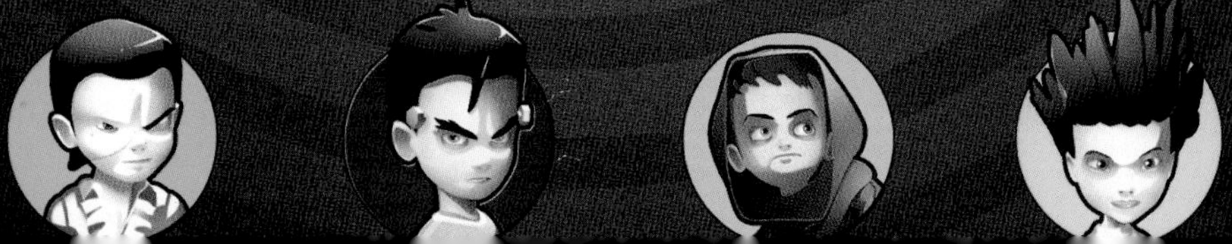

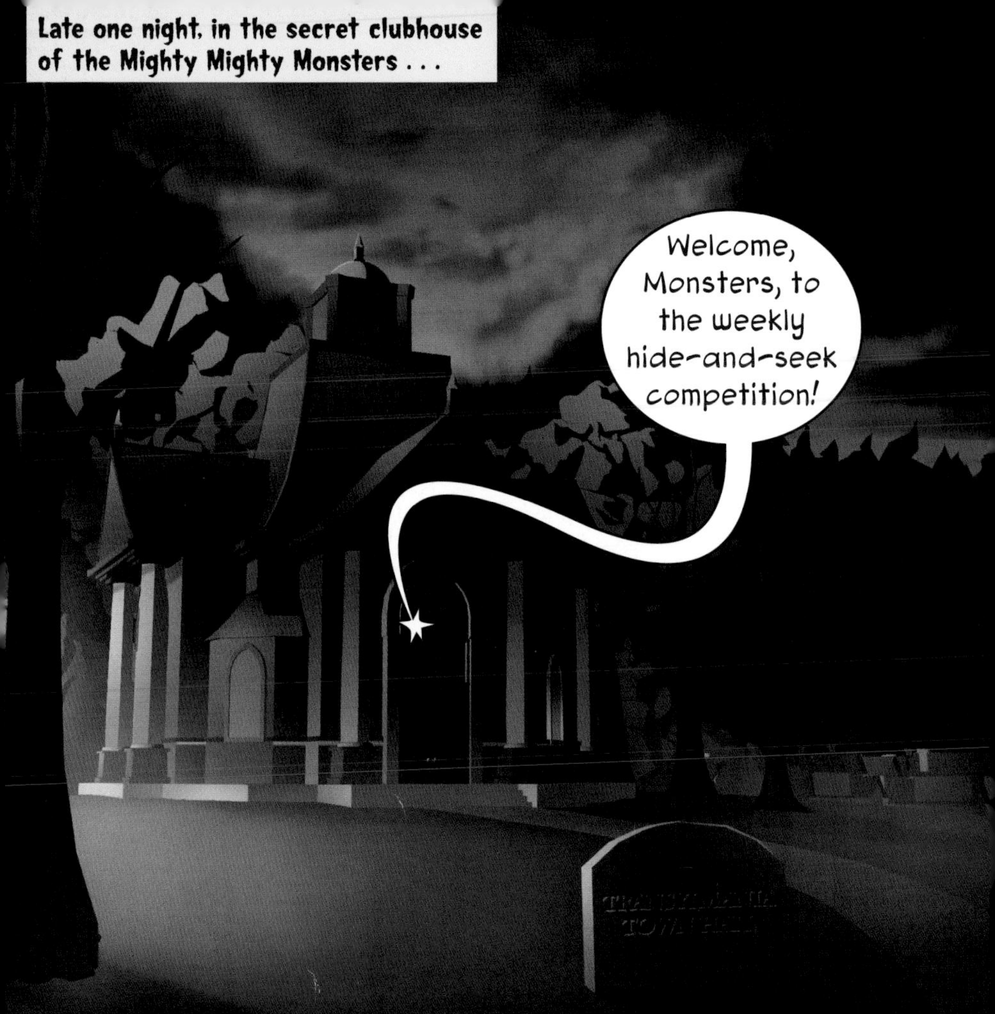
Late one night, in the secret clubhouse of the Mighty Mighty Monsters . . .
Welcome, Monsters, to the weekly hide-and-seek competition!

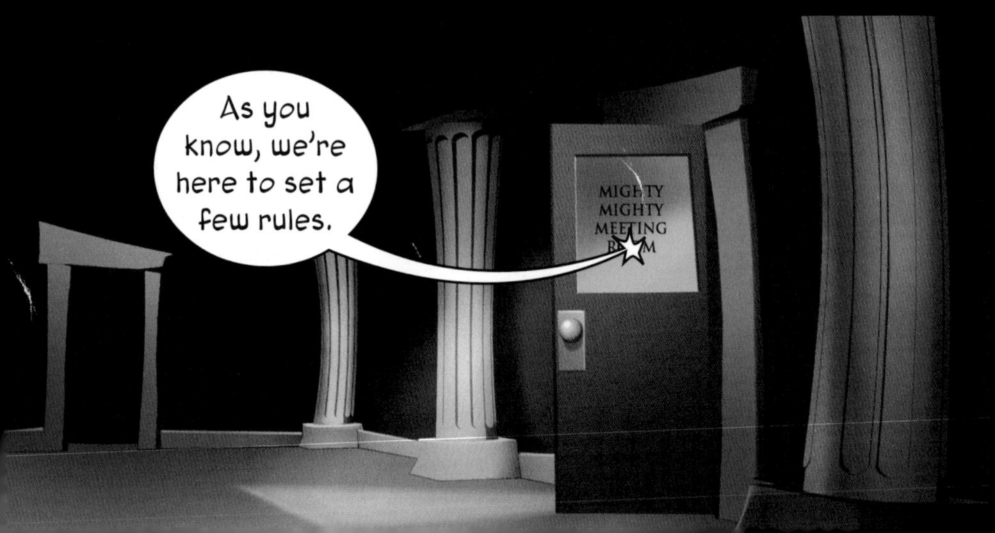
As you know, we're here to set a few rules.

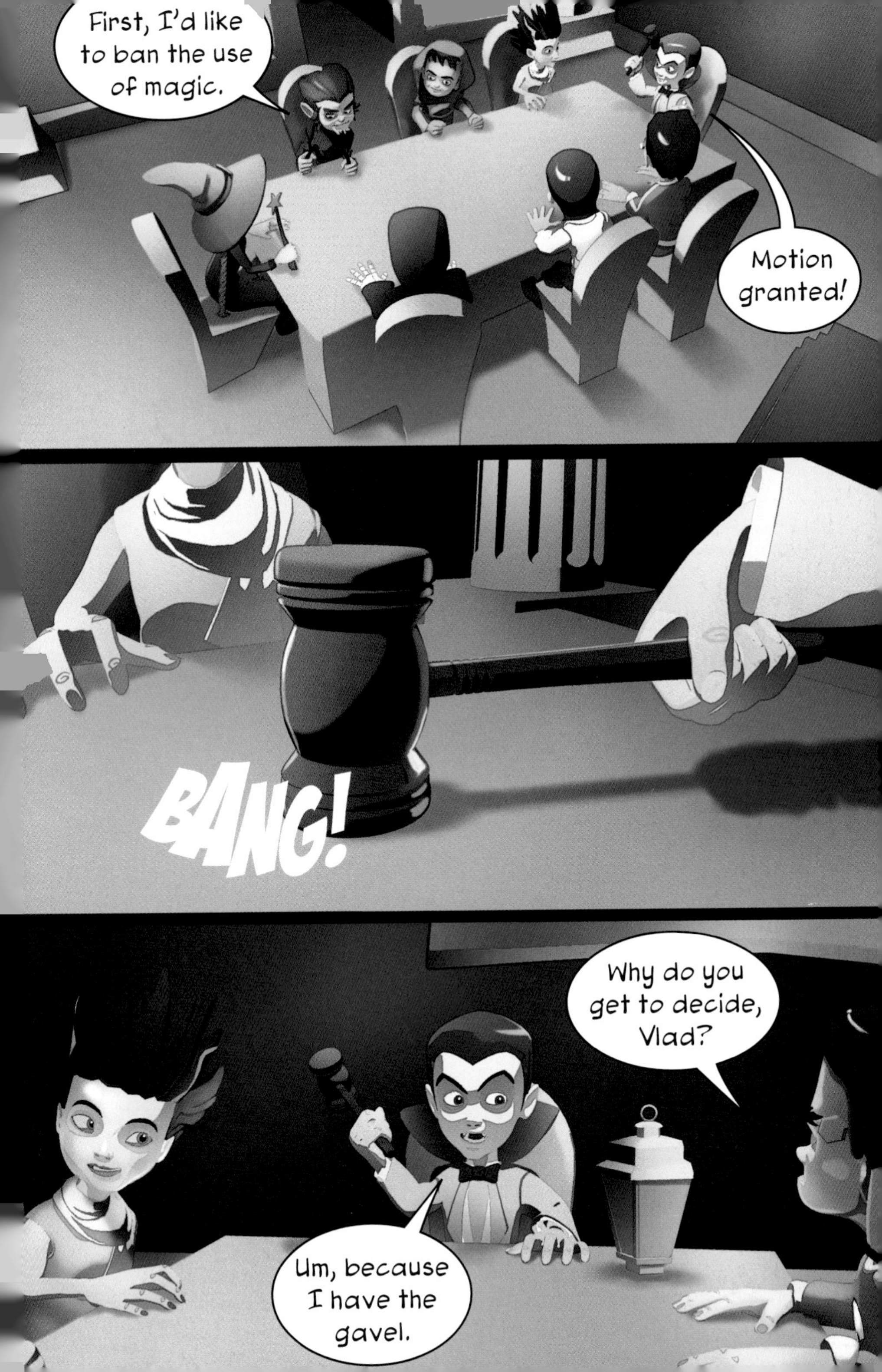
First, I'd like to ban the use of magic.
Motion granted!
BANG!
Why do you get to decide, Vlad?
Um, because I have the gavel.

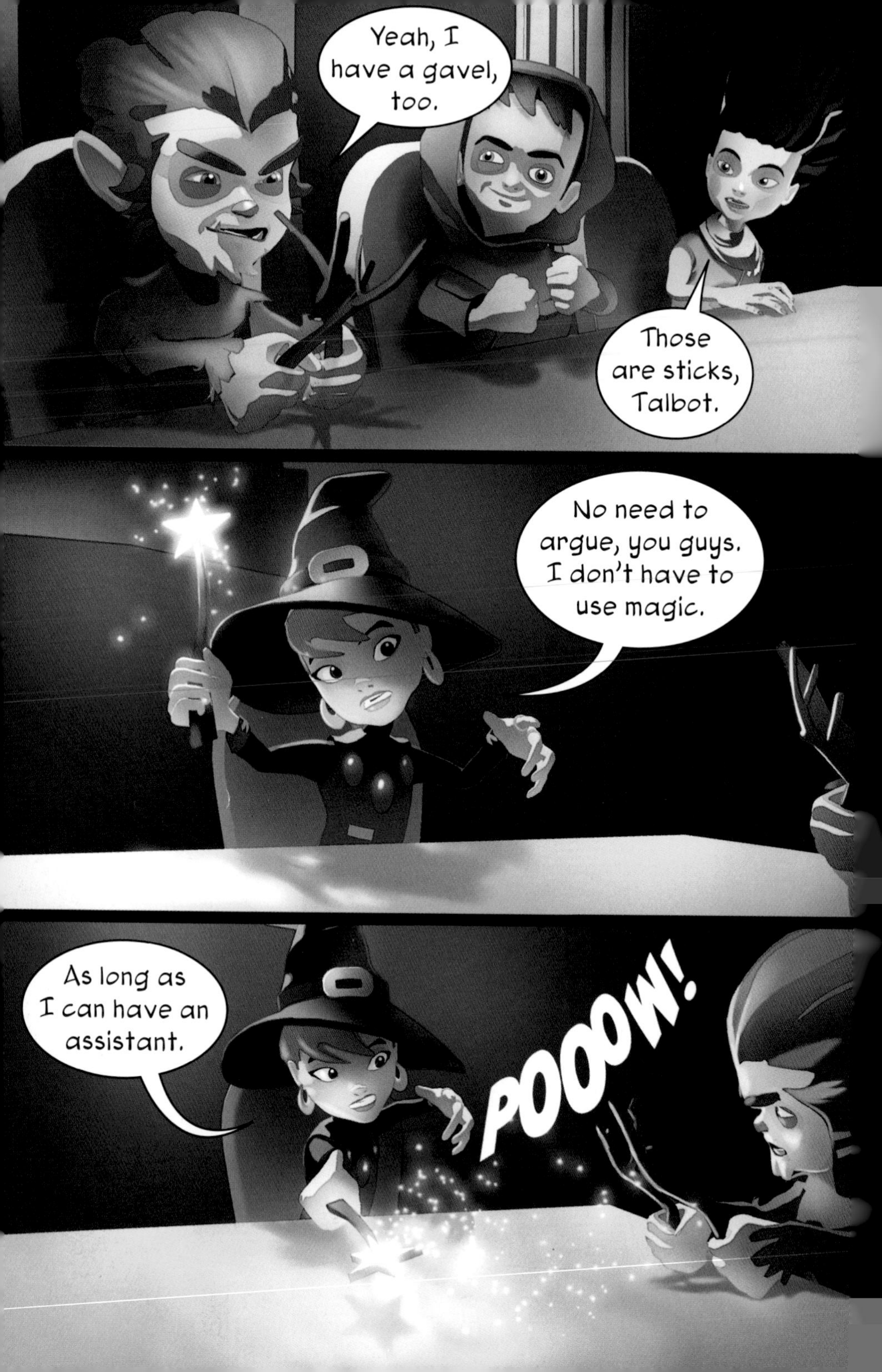
Yeah, I have a gavel, too.
Those are sticks, Talbot.
No need to argue, you guys. I don't have to use magic.
As long as I can have an assistant.
POOOW!

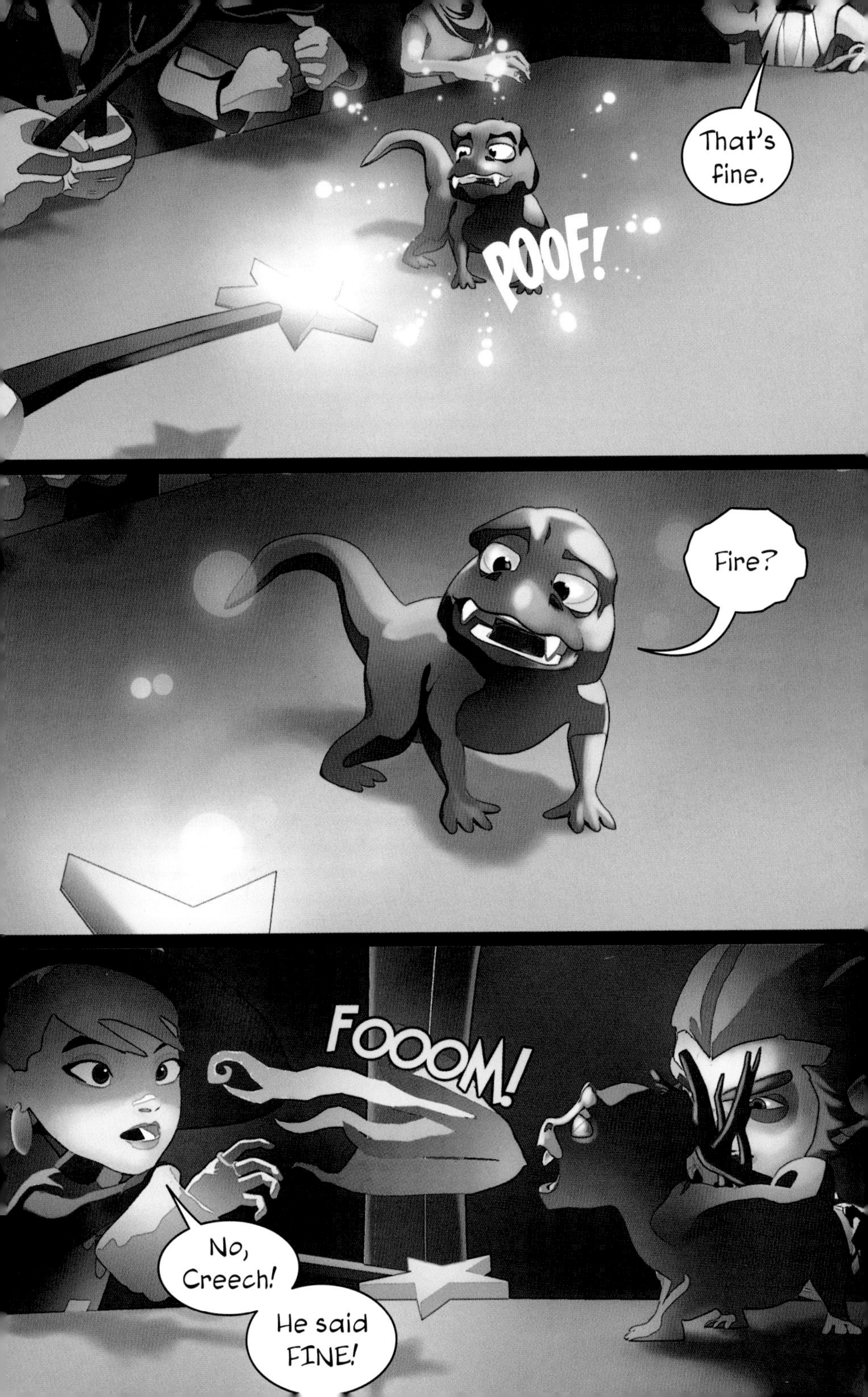
That's fine.
POOF!
Fire?
FOOOM!
No, Creech!
He said FINE!

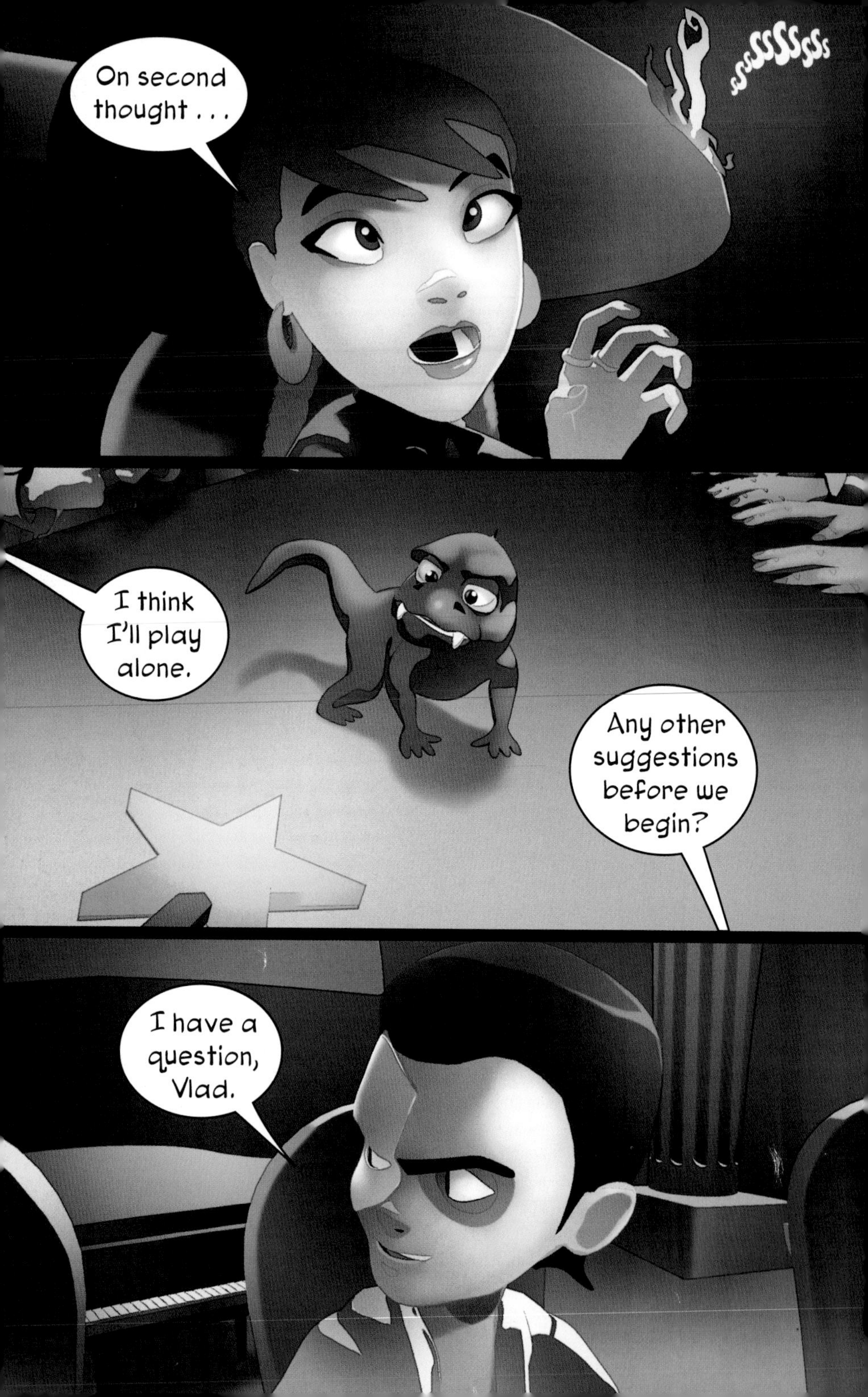
On second thought . . .
sSSSSSsss
I think I'll play alone.
Any other suggestions before we begin?
I have a question, Vlad.

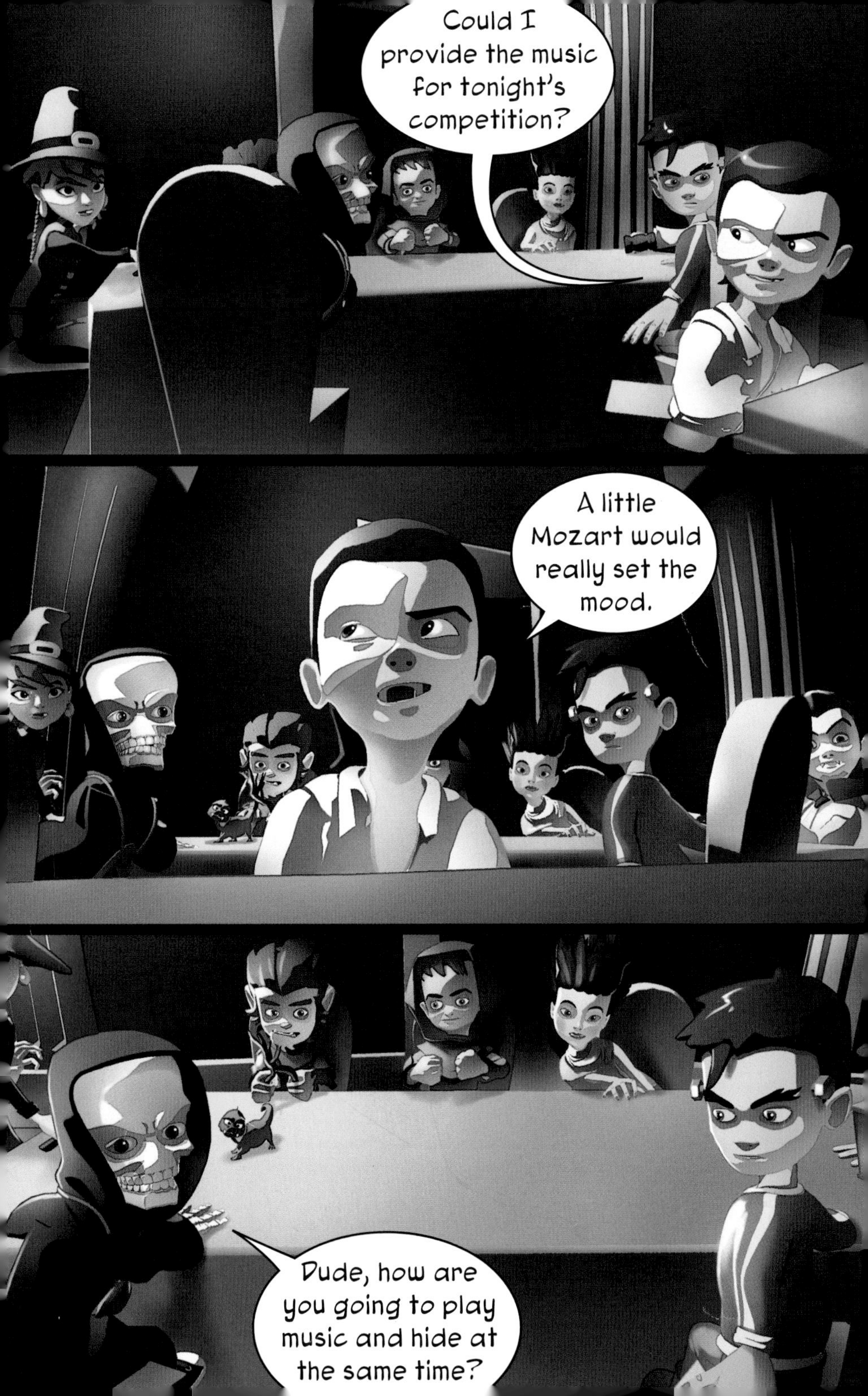
Could I provide the music for tonight's competition?
A little Mozart would really set the mood.
Dude, how are you going to play music and hide at the same time?

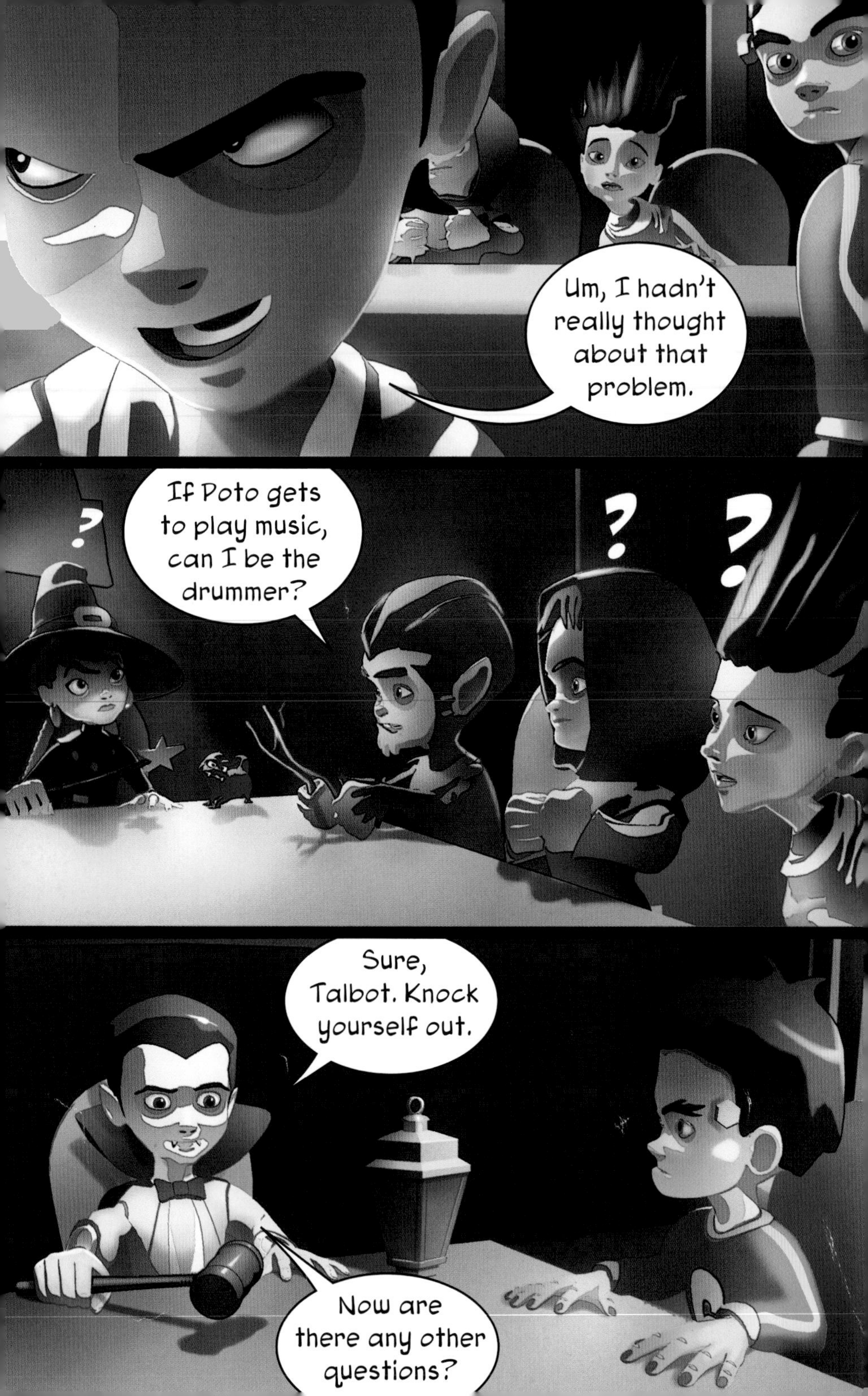
Um, I hadn't really thought about that problem.
If Poto gets to play music, can I be the drummer?
?
?
?
Sure, Talbot. Knock yourself out.
Now are there any other questions?

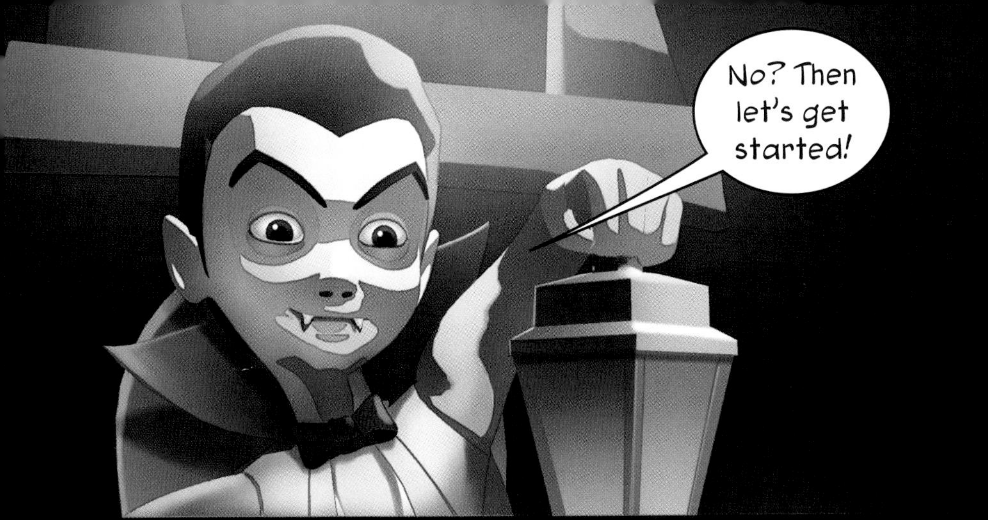
No? Then let's get started!

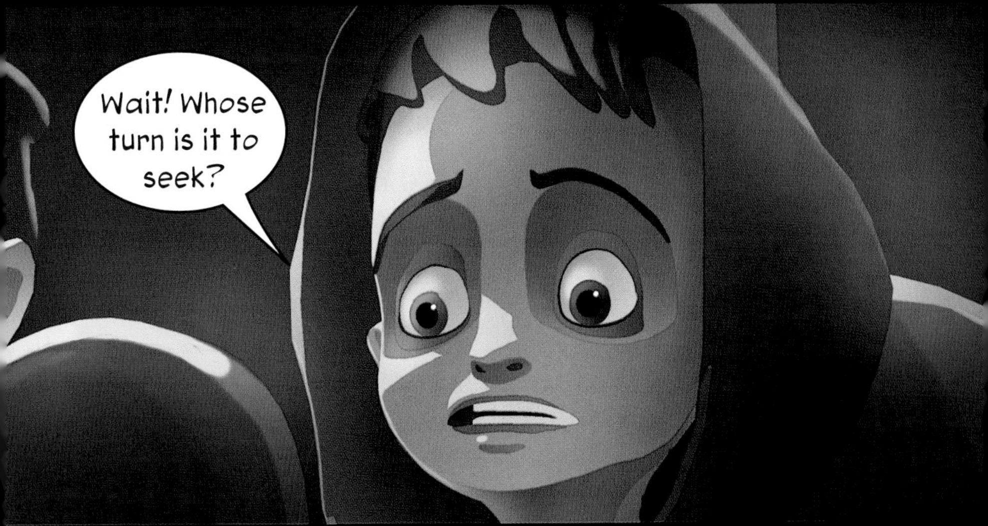
Wait! Whose turn is it to seek?

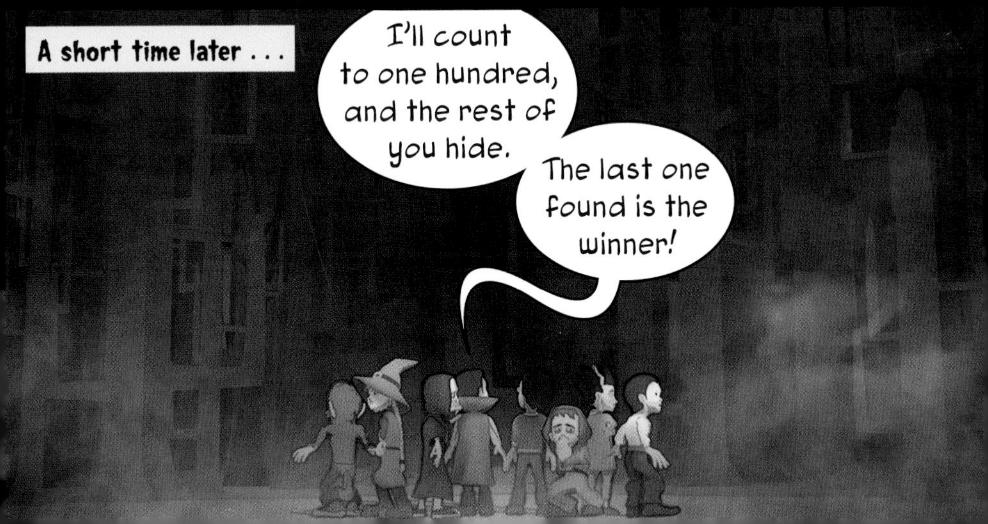
A short time later . . .
I'll count to one hundred, and the rest of you hide.
The last one found is the winner!

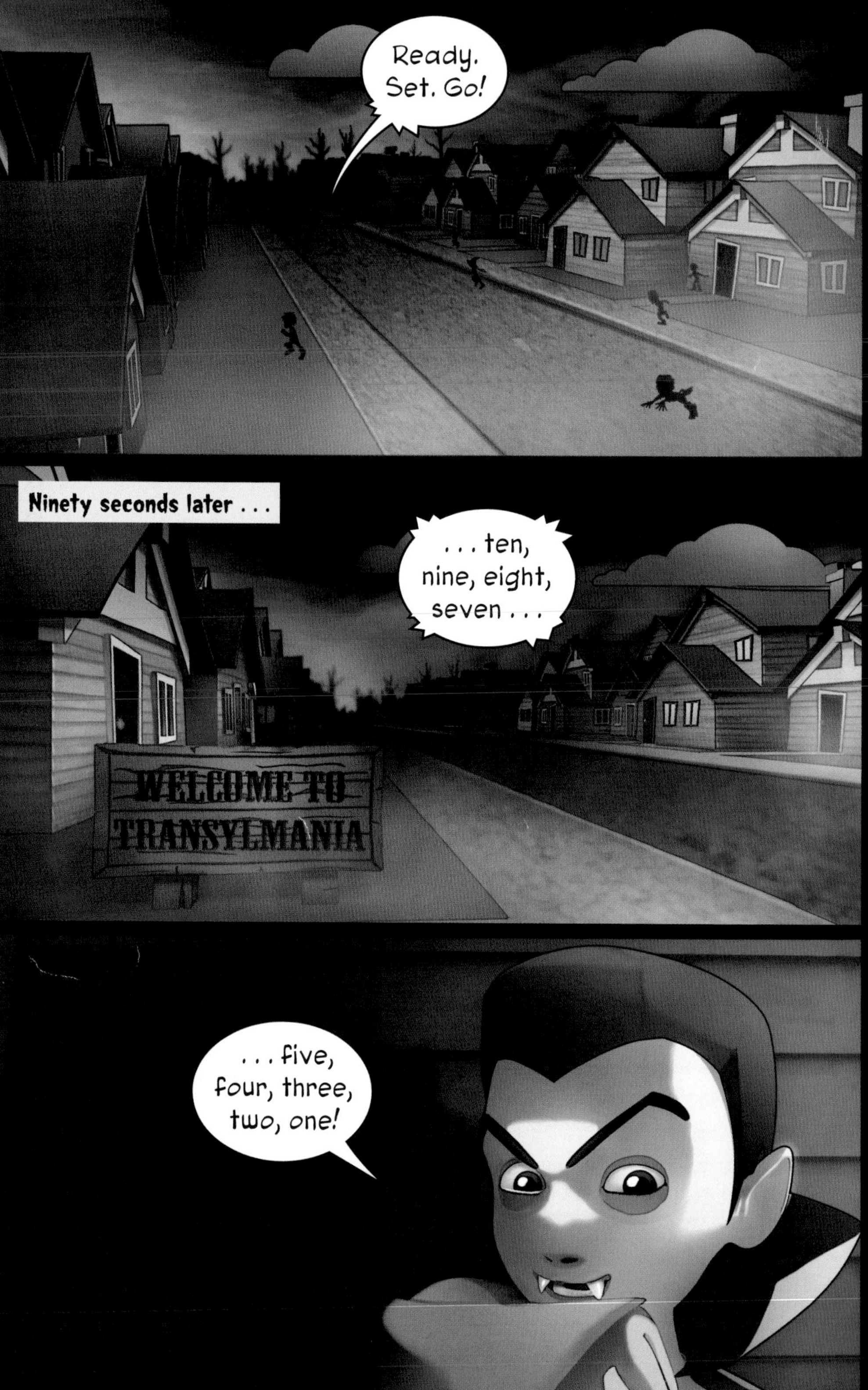
Ready. Set. Go!
Ninety seconds later . . .
. . . ten, nine, eight, seven . . .
WELCOME TO TRANSYLMANIA
. . . five, four, three, two, one!

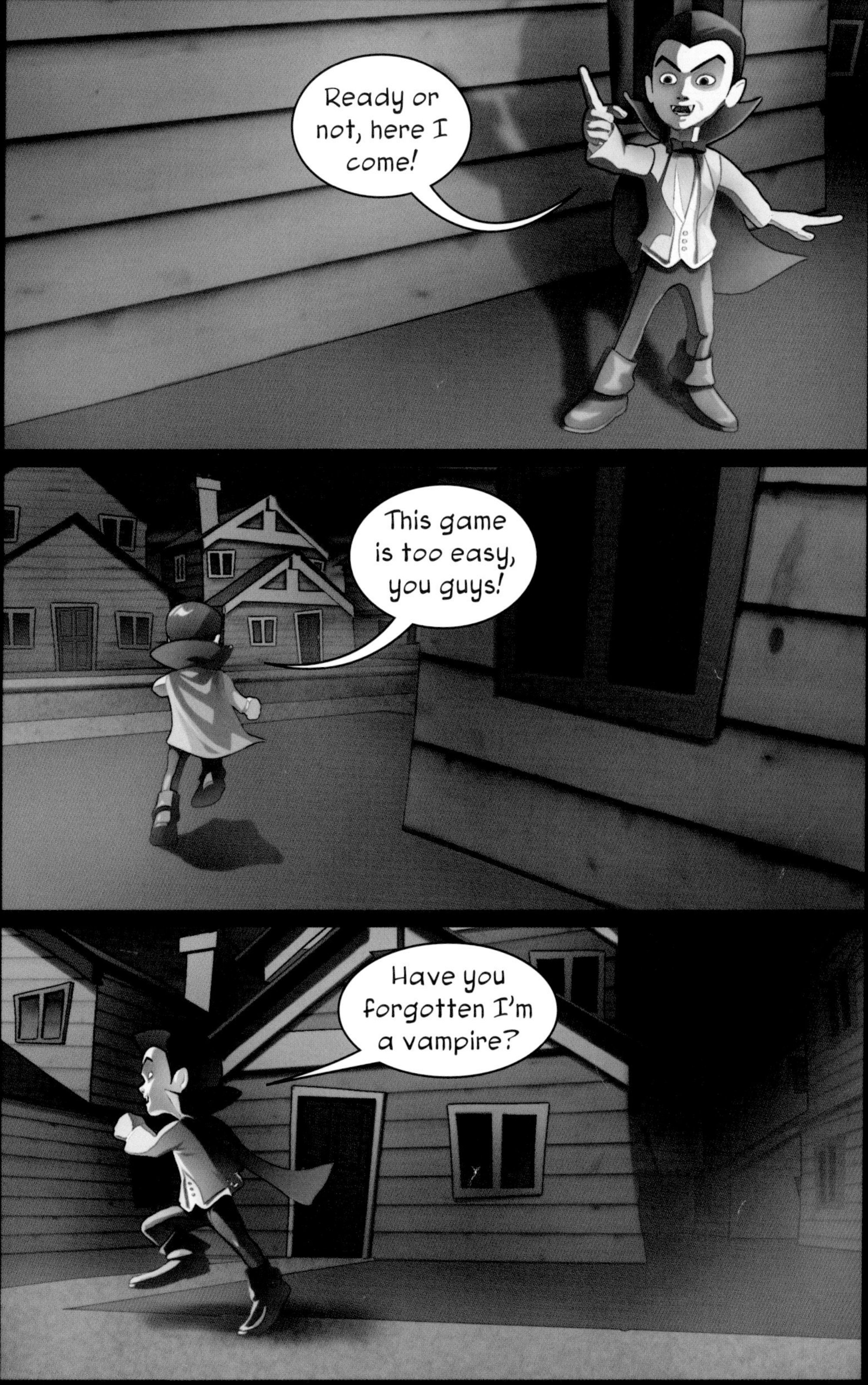
Ready or not, here I come!
This game is too easy, you guys!
Have you forgotten I'm a vampire?

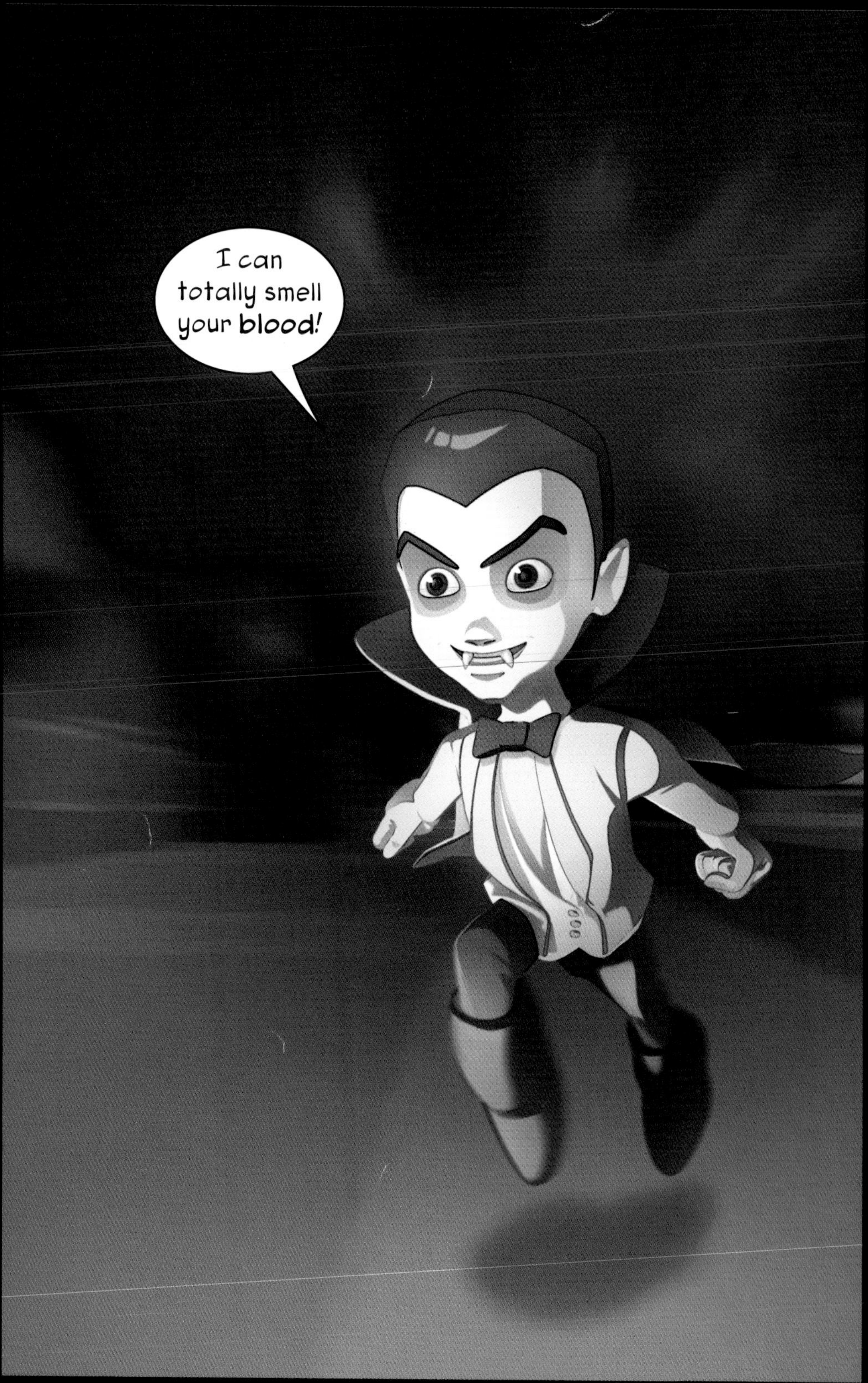
I can totally smell your **blood**!

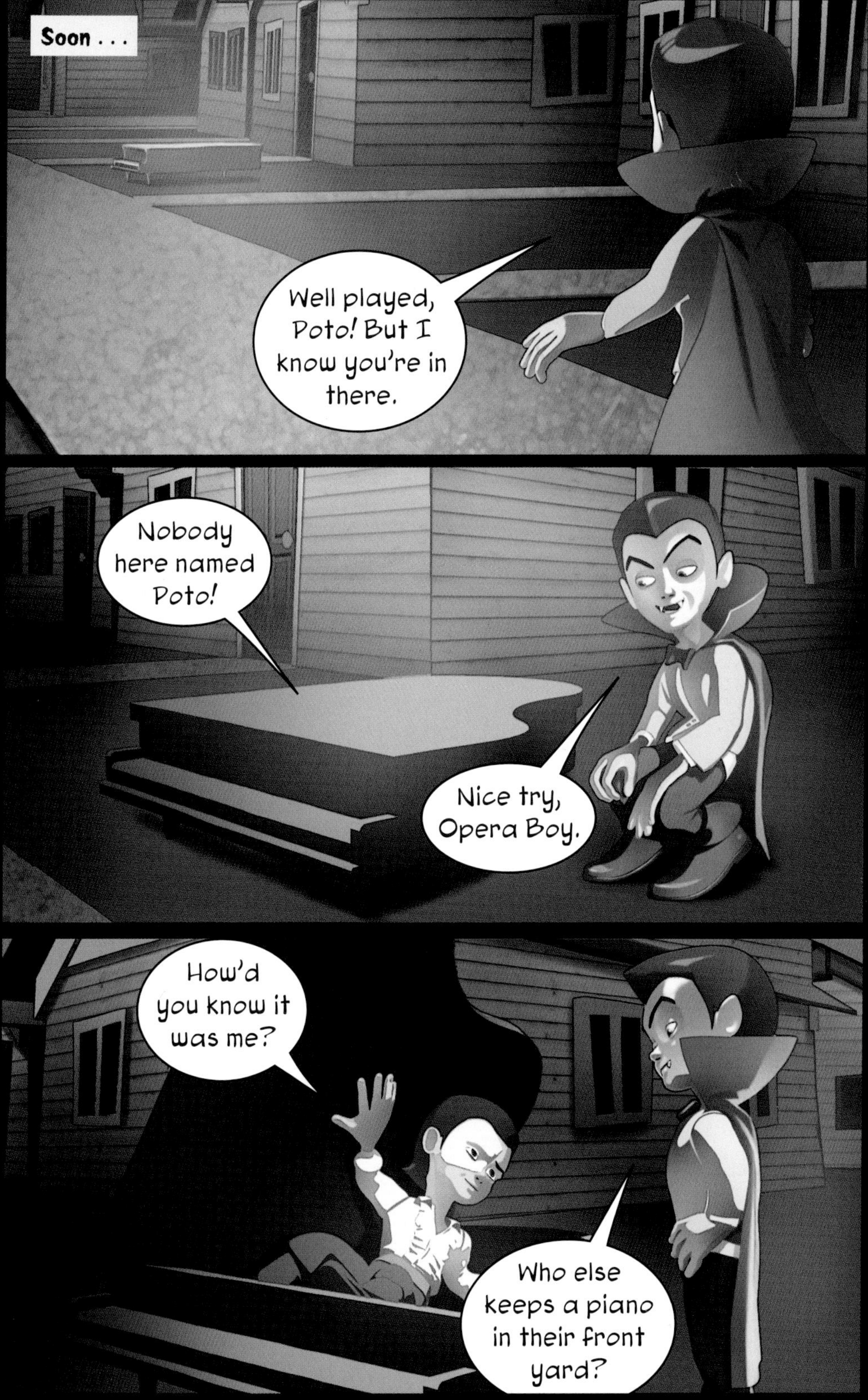
Soon . . .
Well played, Poto! But I know you're in there.
Nobody here named Poto!
Nice try, Opera Boy.
How'd you know it was me?
Who else keeps a piano in their front yard?

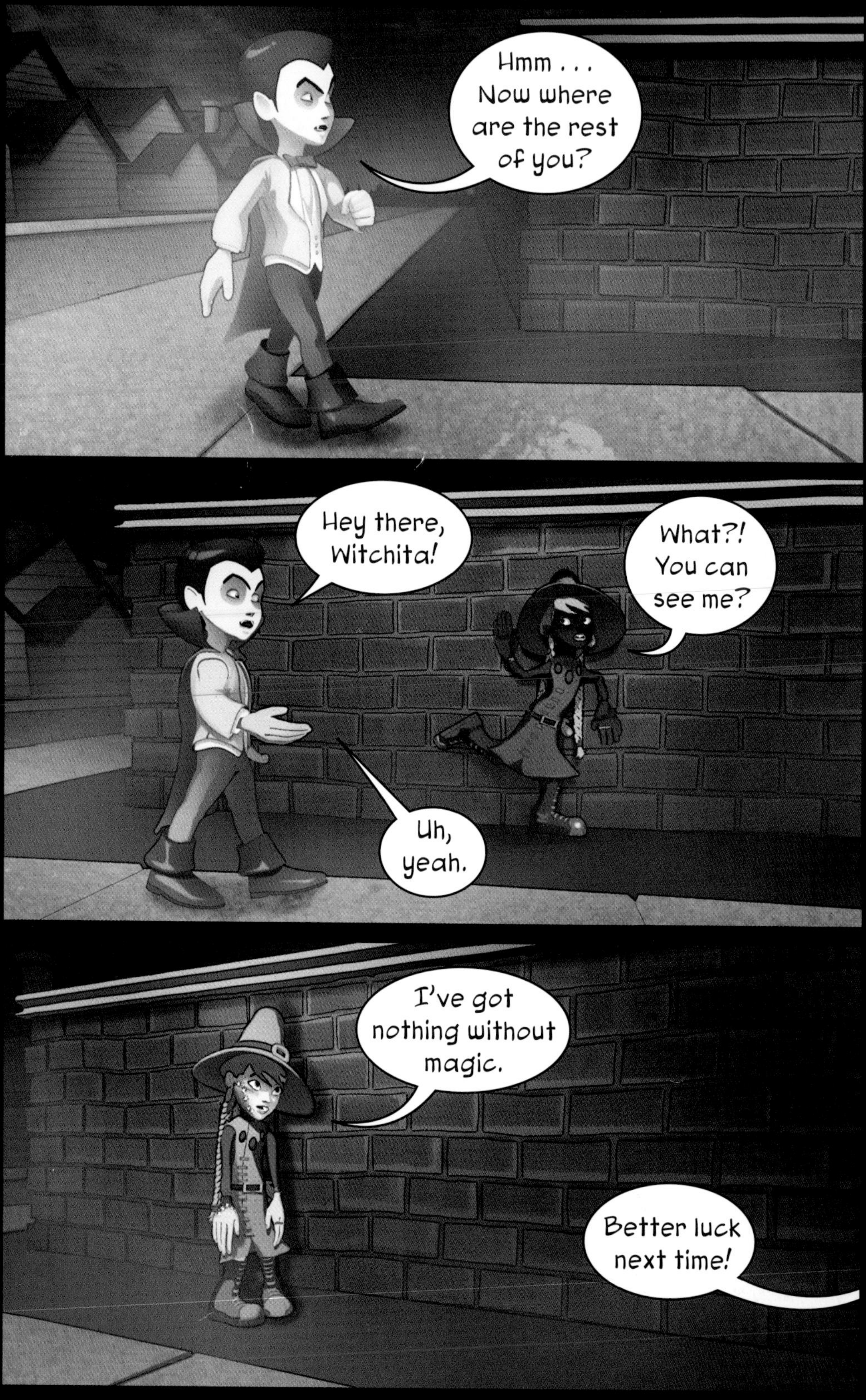
Hmm . . .
Now where are the rest of you?
Hey there, Witchita!
What?! You can see me?
Uh, yeah.
I've got nothing without magic.
Better luck next time!

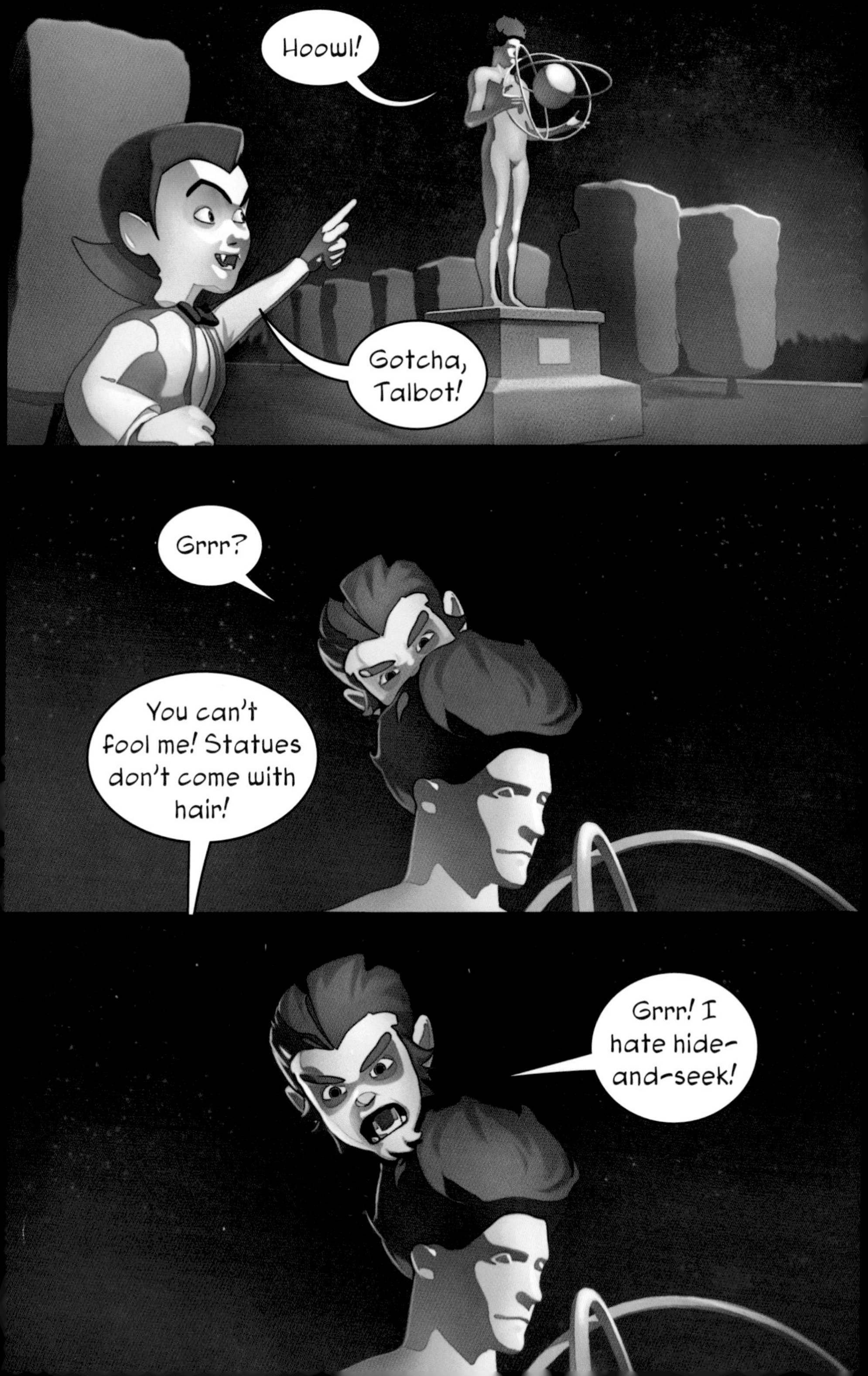
Hoowl!
Gotcha, Talbot!
Grrr?
You can't fool me! Statues don't come with hair!
Grrr! I hate hide-and-seek!

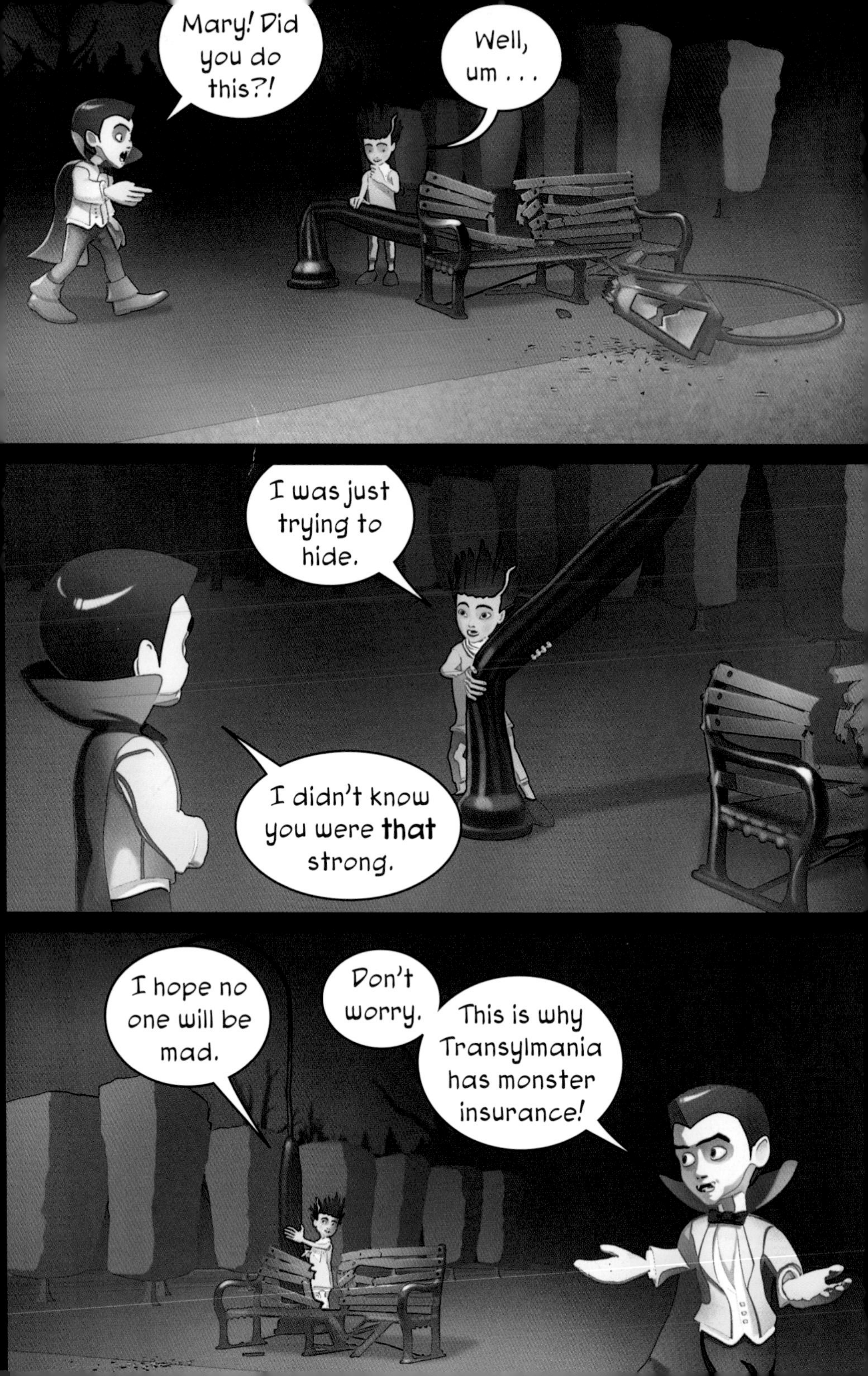
Mary! Did you do this?!
Well, um . . .
I was just trying to hide.
I didn't know you were **that** strong.
I hope no one will be mad.
Don't worry.
This is why Transylmania has monster insurance!

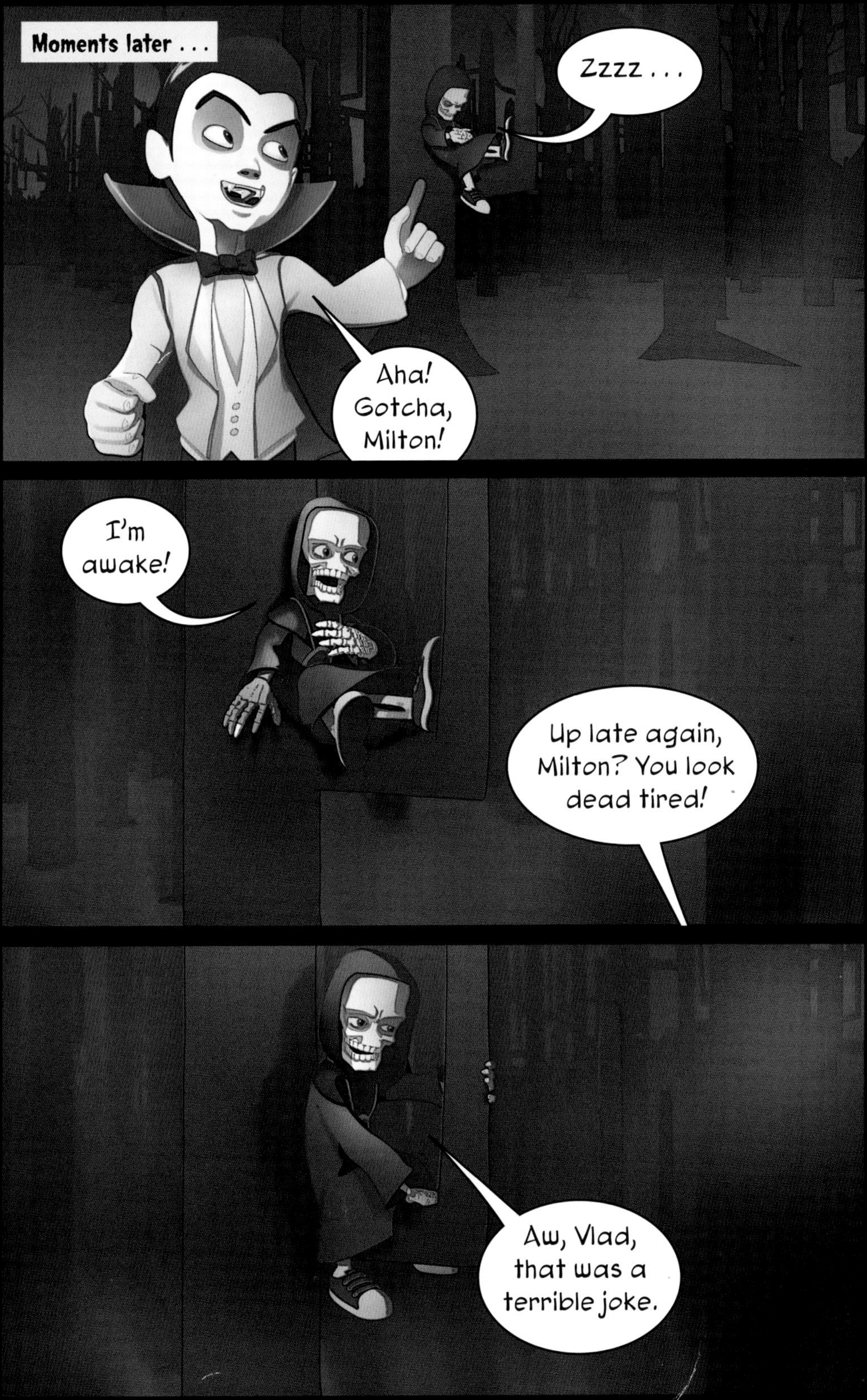
Moments later . . .
Zzzz . . .
Aha! Gotcha, Milton!
I'm awake!
Up late again, Milton? You look dead tired!
Aw, Vlad, that was a terrible joke.

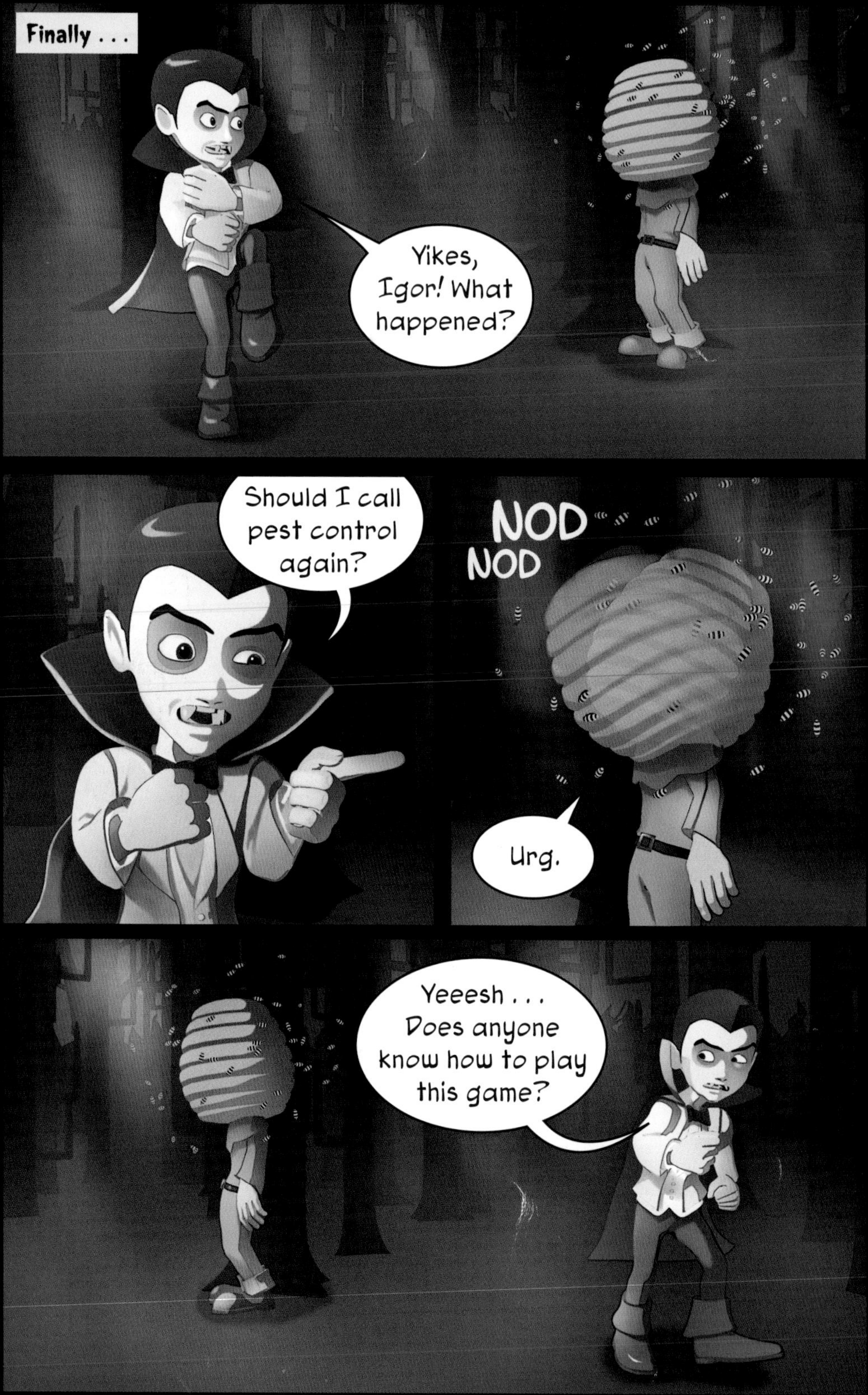
Finally . . .
Yikes, Igor! What happened?
Should I call pest control again?
NOD
NOD
Urg.
Yeeesh . . . Does anyone know how to play this game?

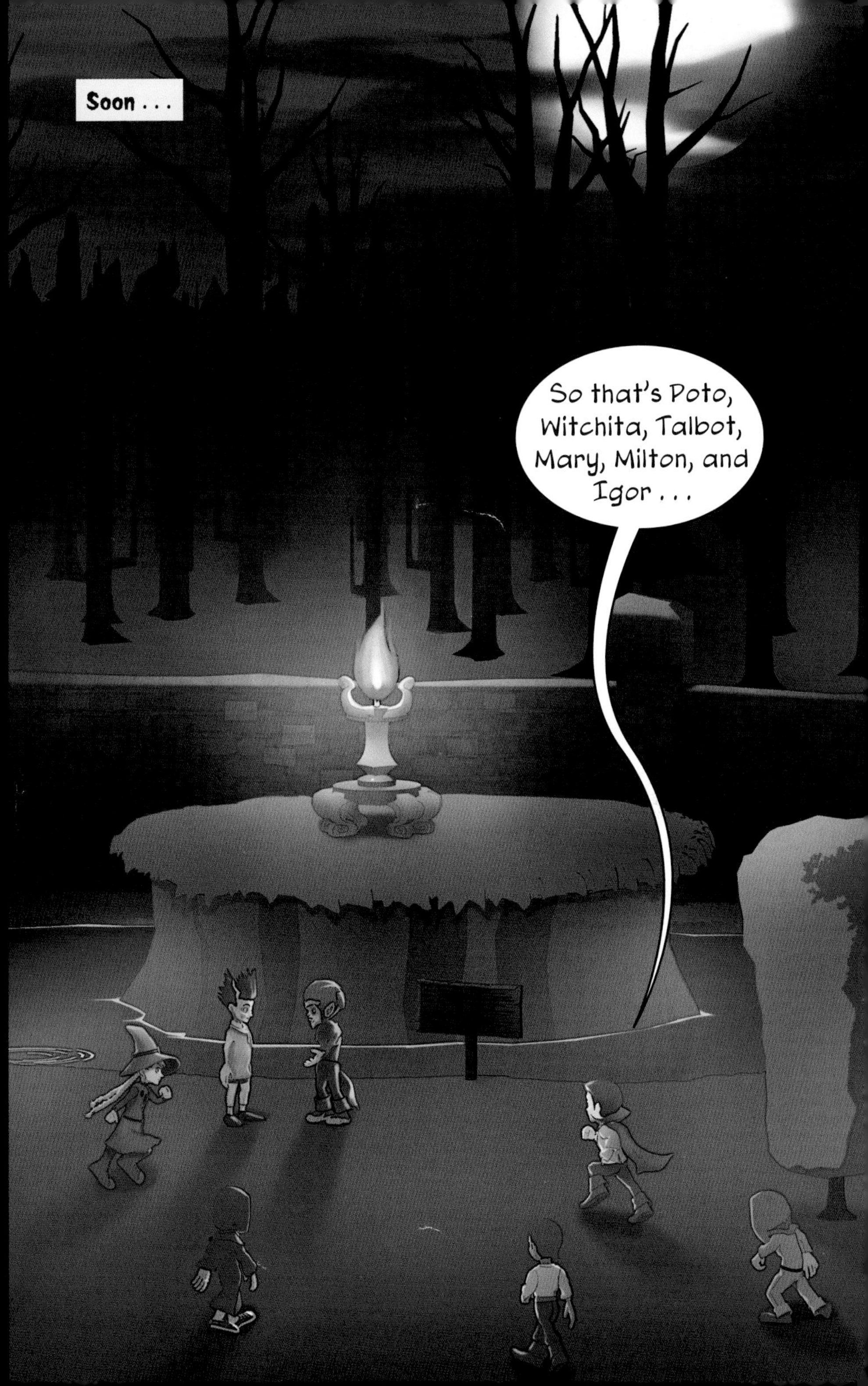
Soon . . .
So that's Poto, Witchita, Talbot, Mary, Milton, and Igor . . .

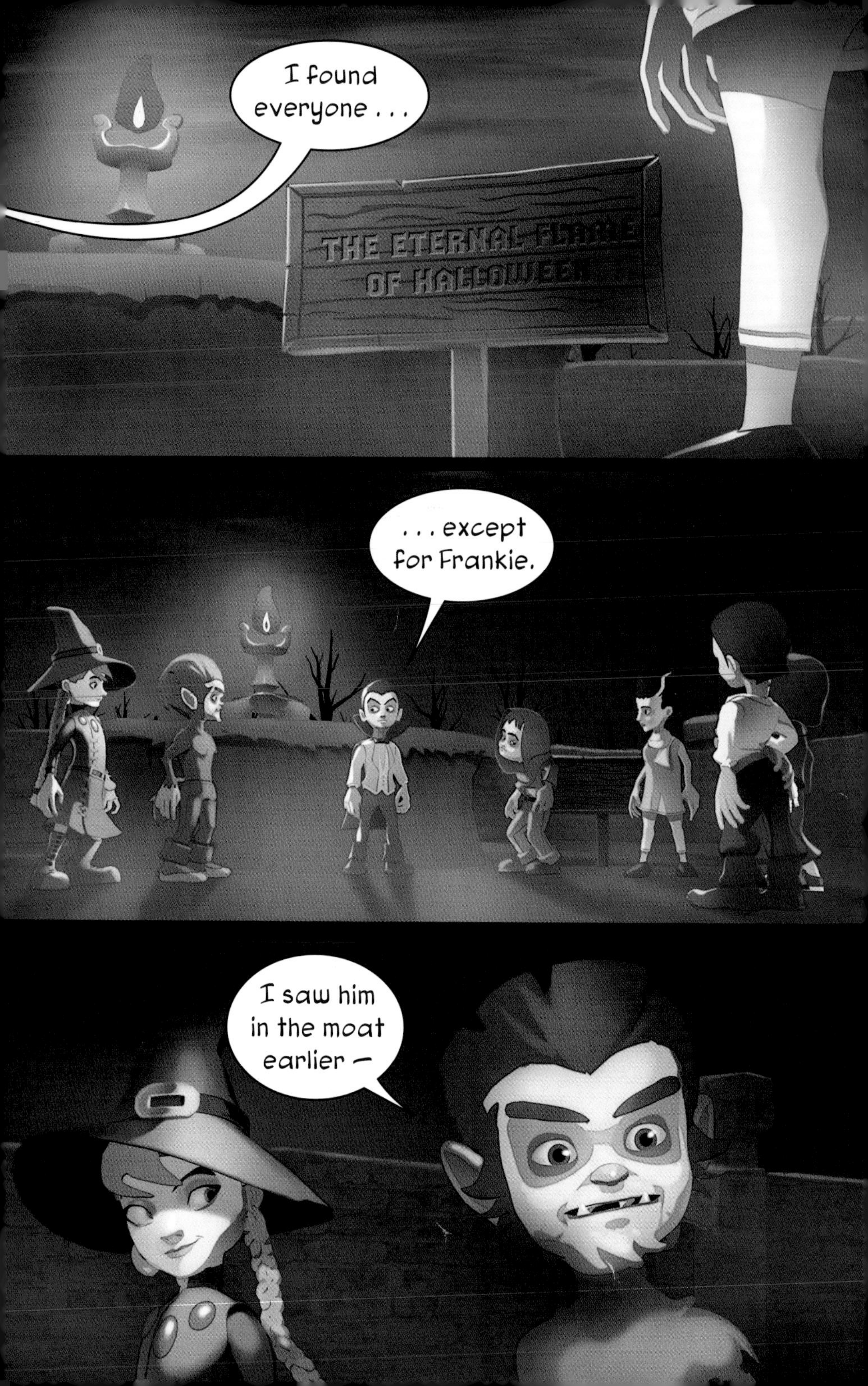
I found everyone . . .
THE ETERNAL FLAME
OF HALLOWEEN
. . . except for Frankie.
I saw him in the moat earlier —

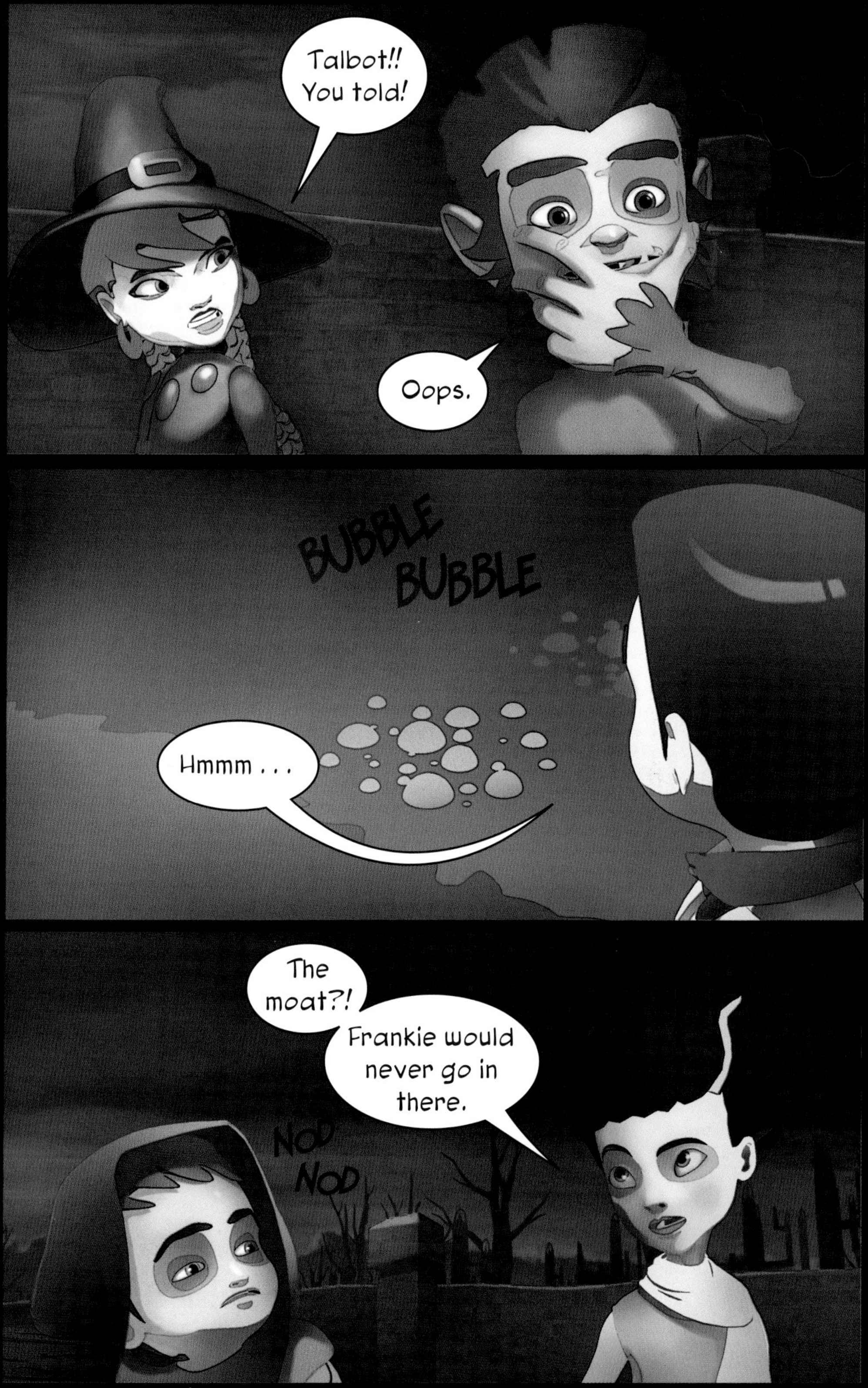
Talbot!! You told!
Oops.
BUBBLE BUBBLE
Hmmm . . .
The moat?!
Frankie would never go in there.
NOD NOD

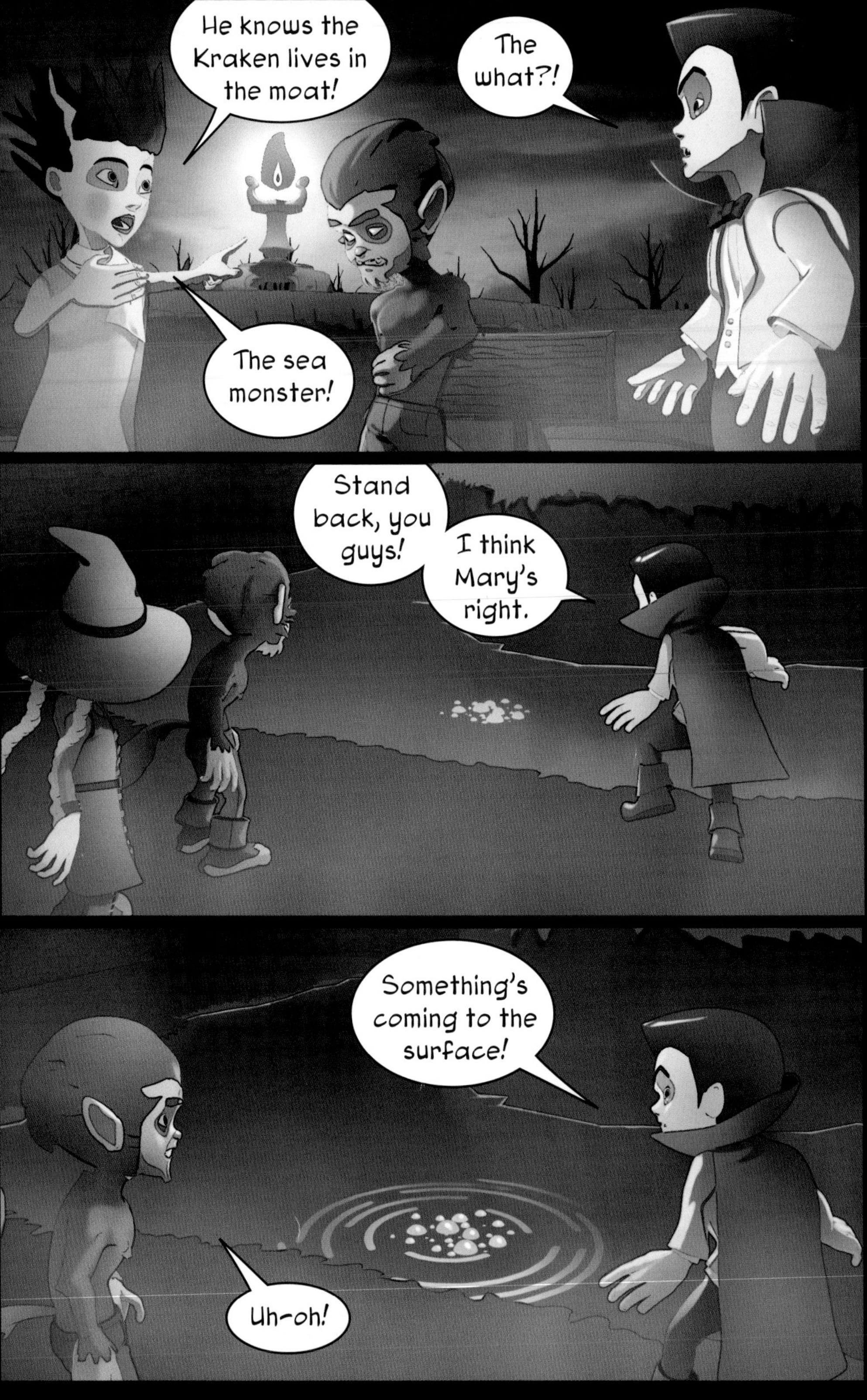
He knows the Kraken lives in the moat!
The what?!
The sea monster!
Stand back, you guys!
I think Mary's right.
Something's coming to the surface!
Uh-oh!

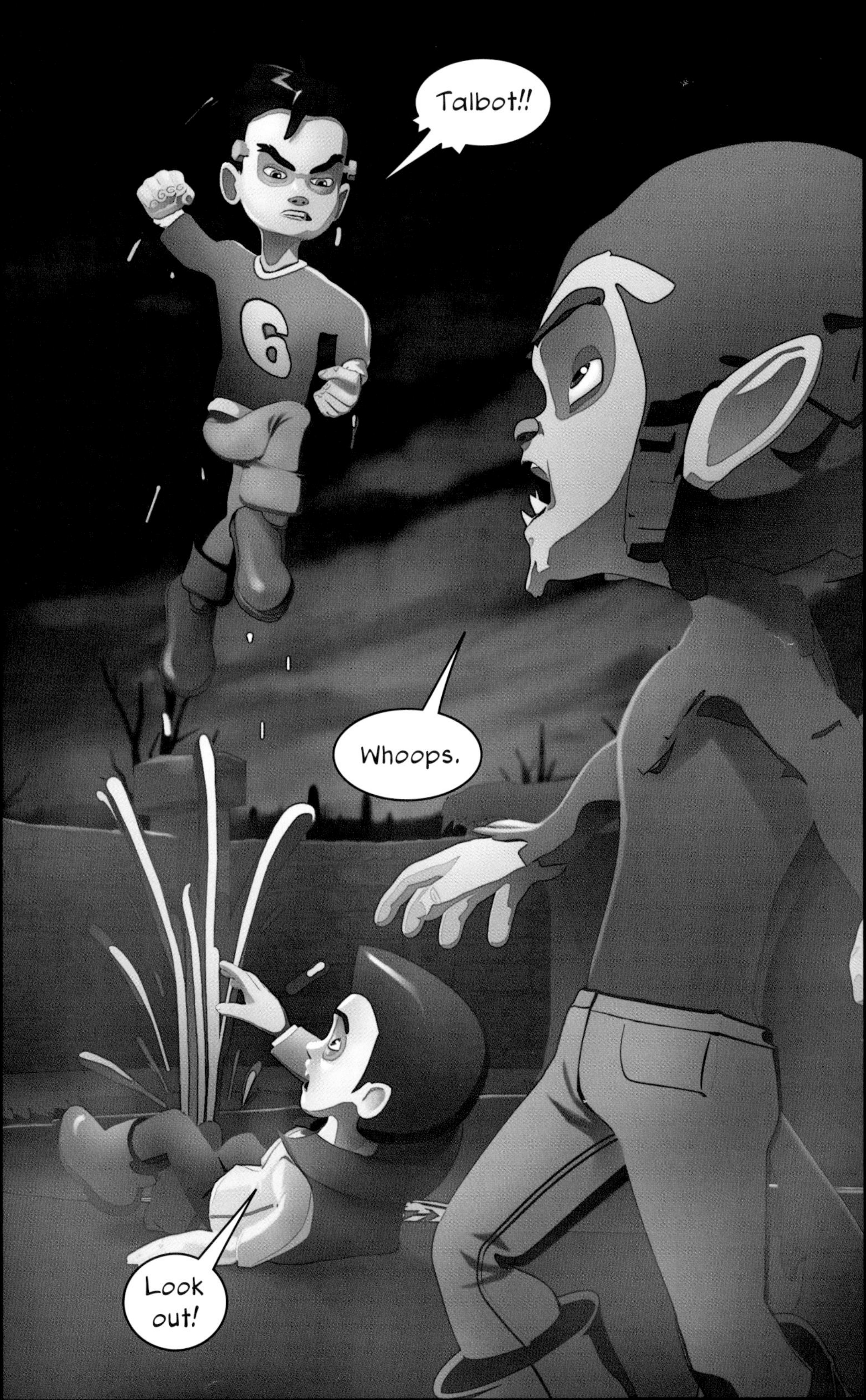
Talbot!!
Whoops.
Look out!

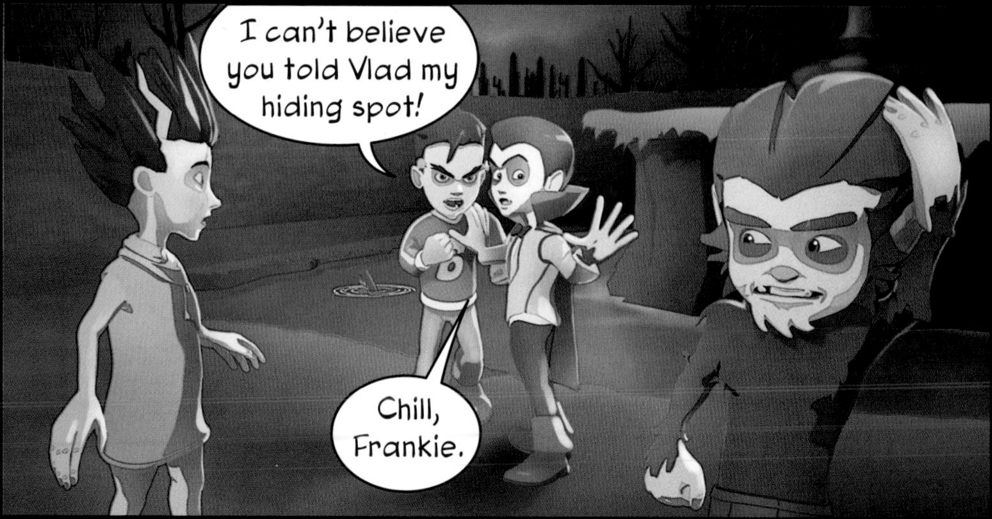
I can't believe you told Vlad my hiding spot!
Chill, Frankie.

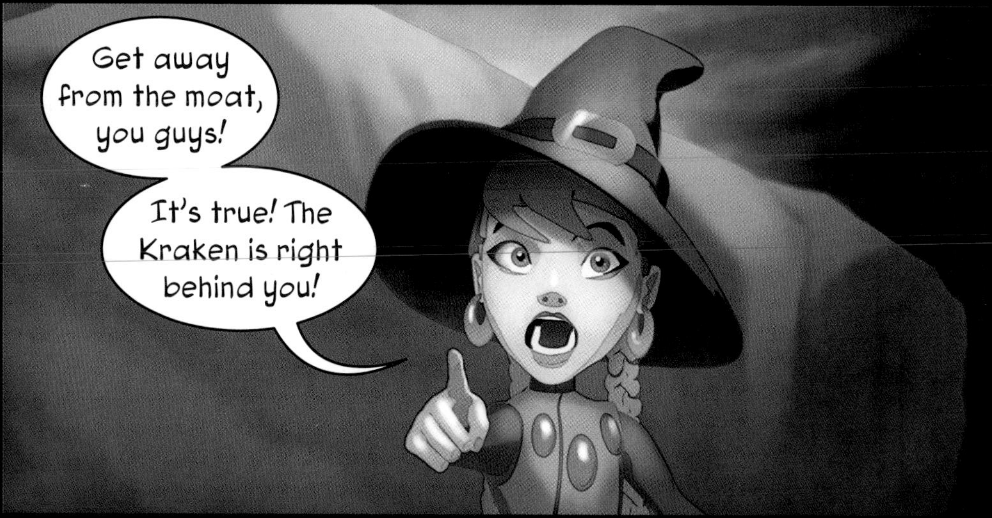
Get away from the moat, you guys!
It's true! The Kraken is right behind you!

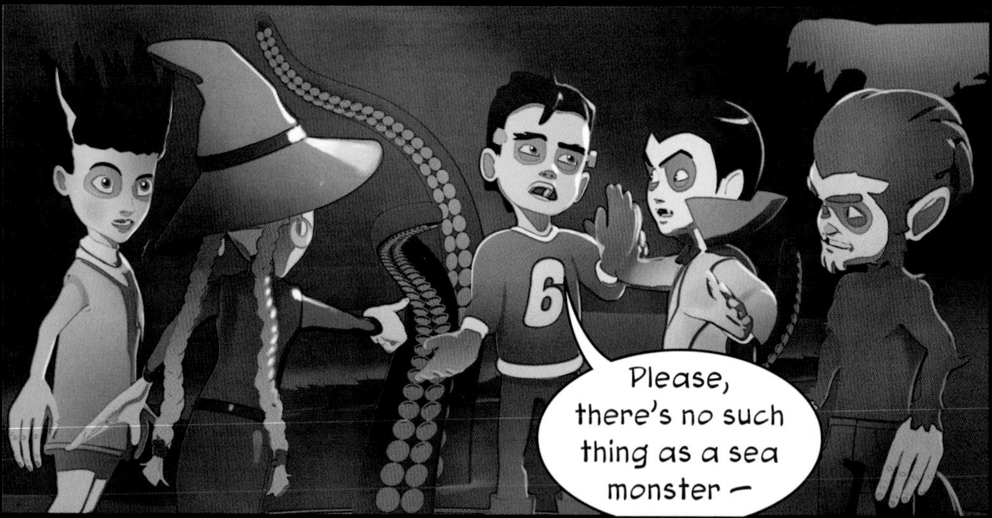
Please, there's no such thing as a sea monster —

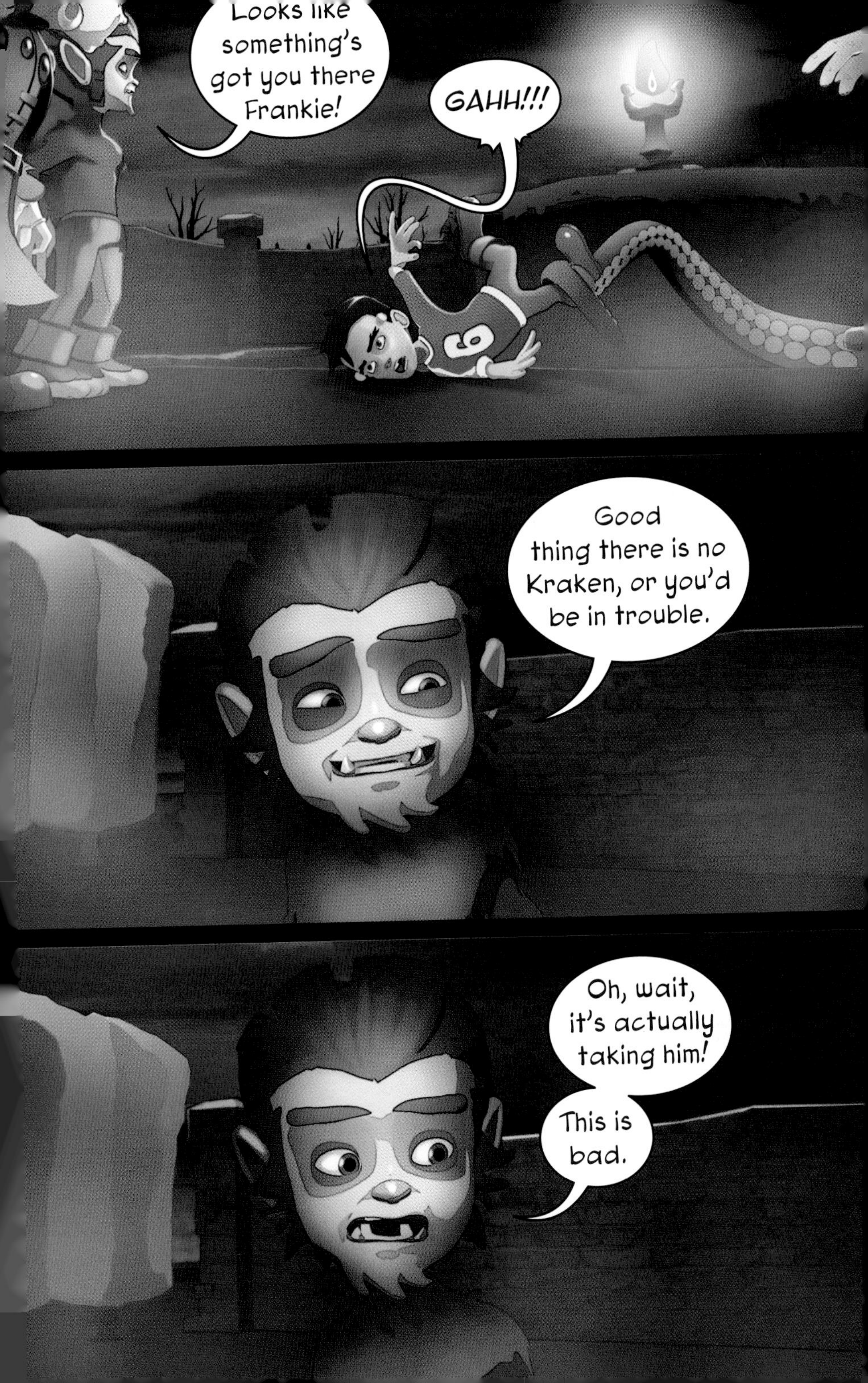
Looks like something's got you there Frankie!
GAHH!!!
Good thing there is no Kraken, or you'd be in trouble.
Oh, wait, it's actually taking him!
This is bad.

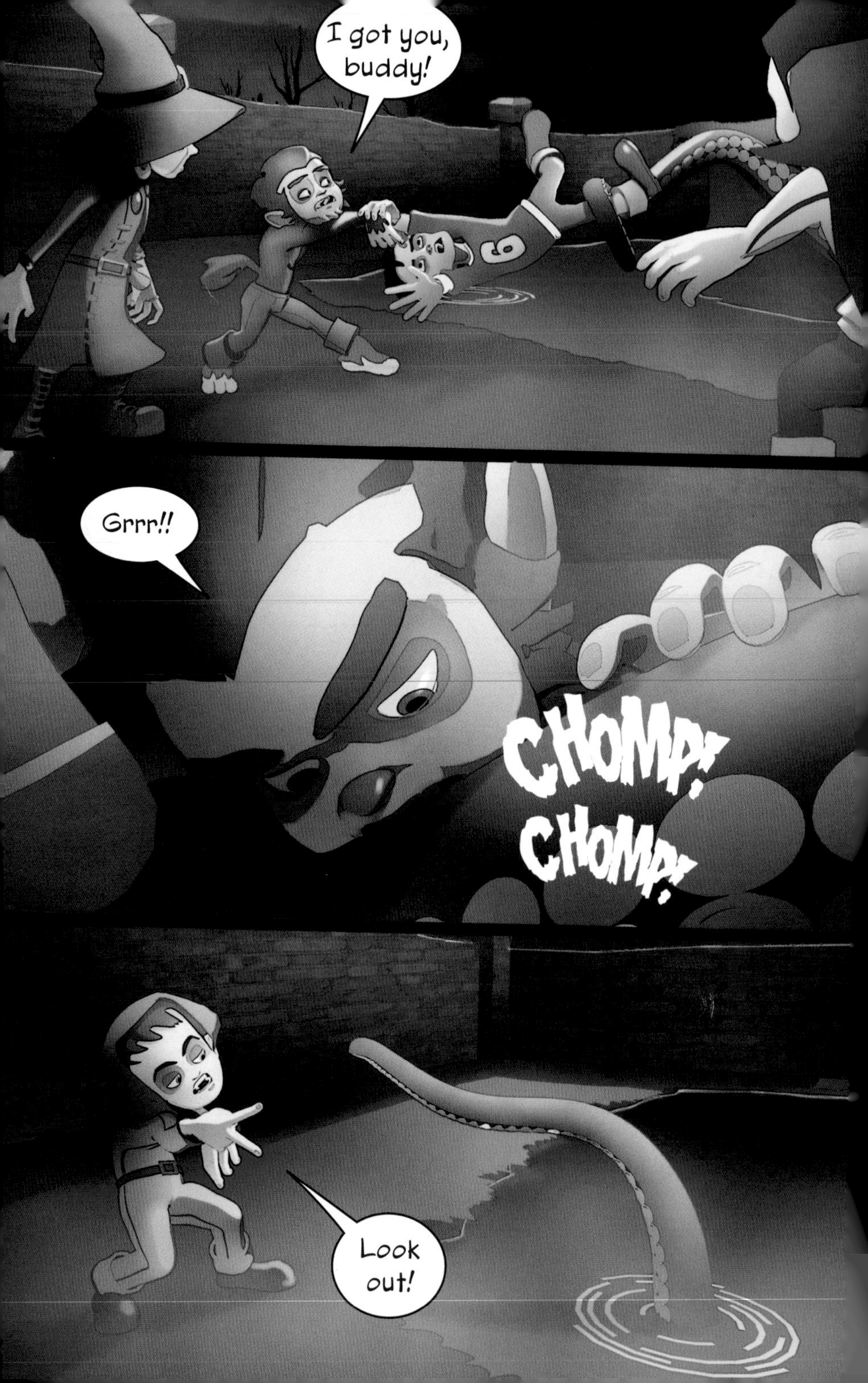
I got you, buddy!
Grrr!!
CHOMP! CHOMP!
Look out!

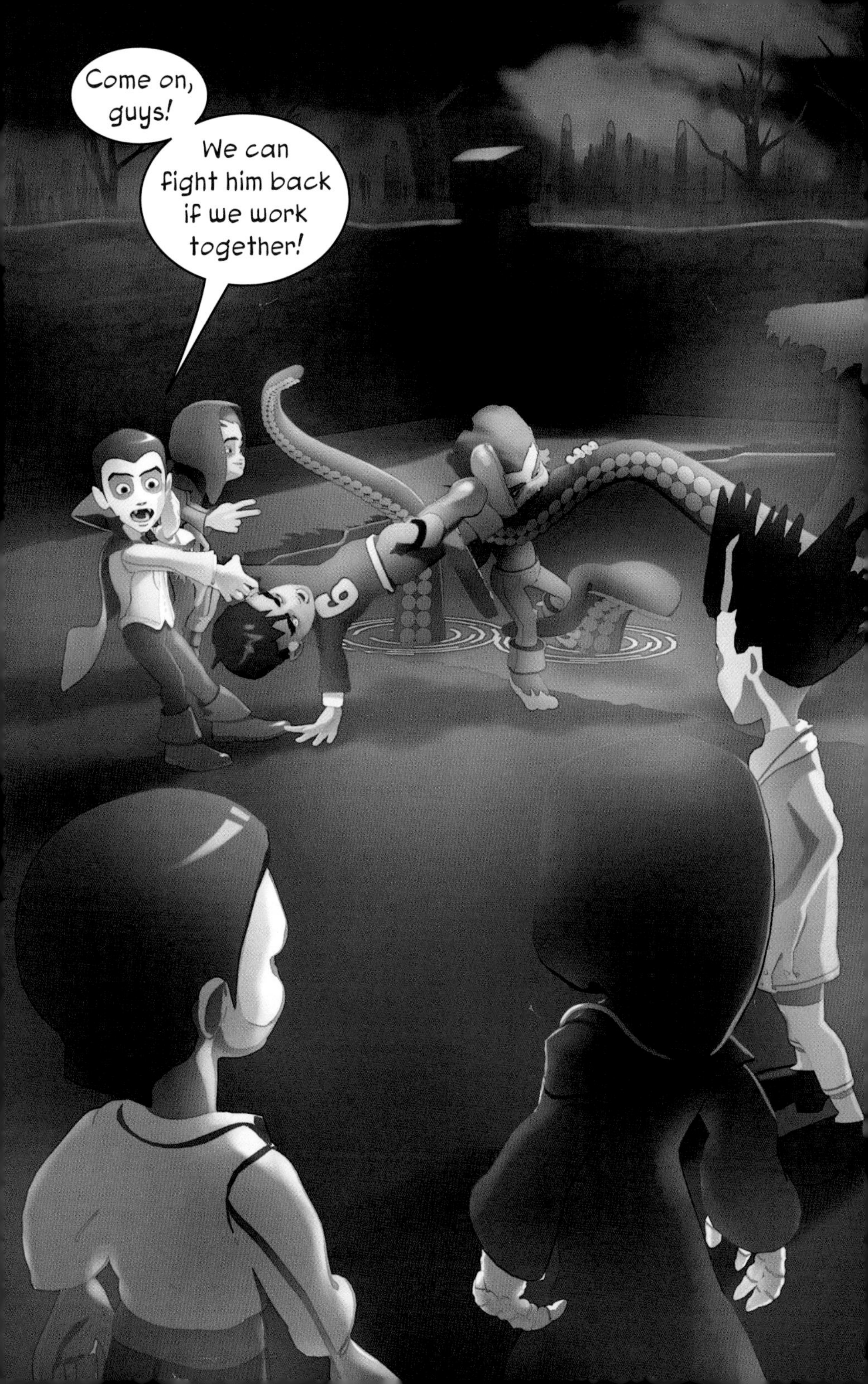
Come on, guys!
We can fight him back if we work together!

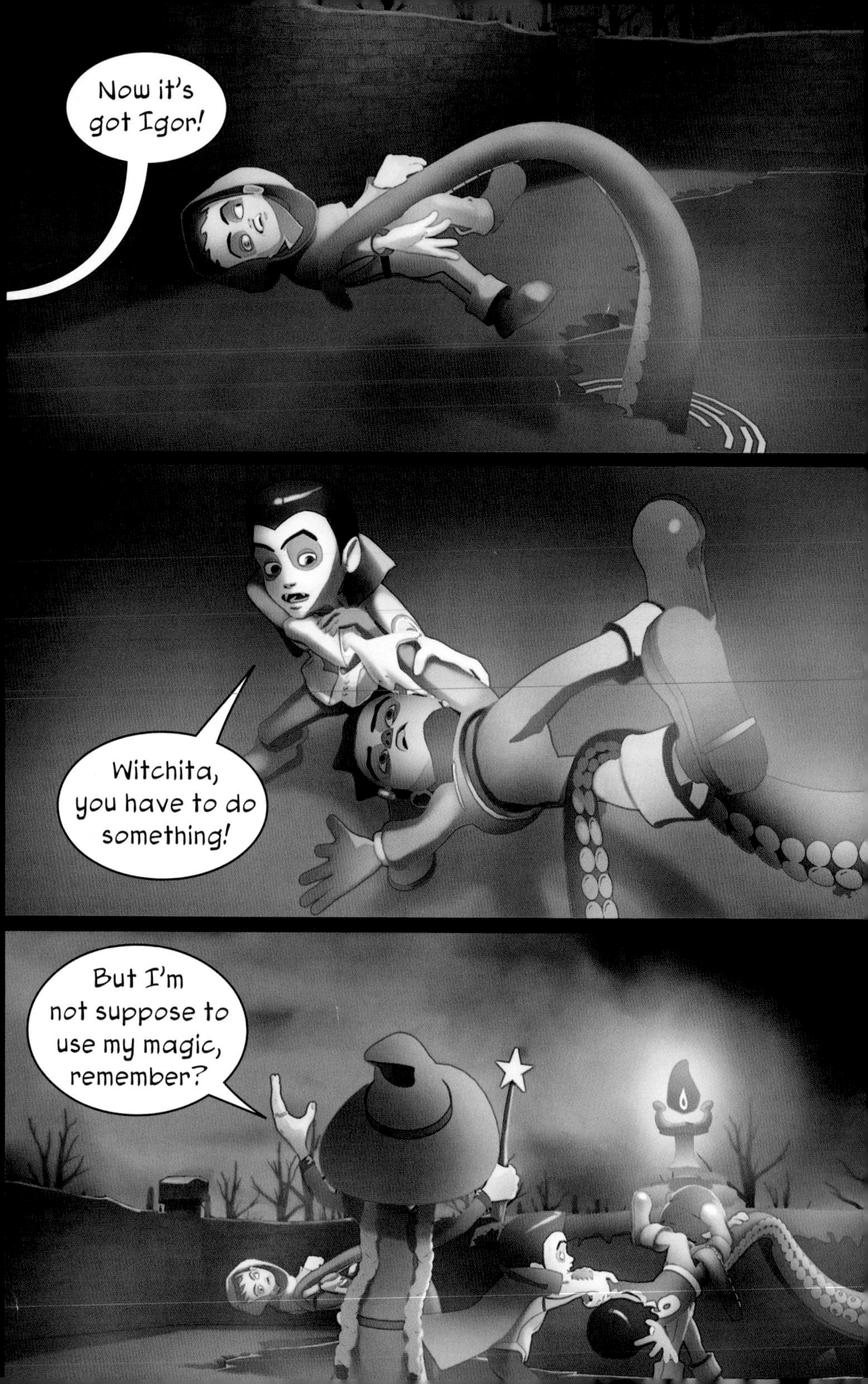
Now it's got Igor!
Witchita, you have to do something!
But I'm not suppose to use my magic, remember?

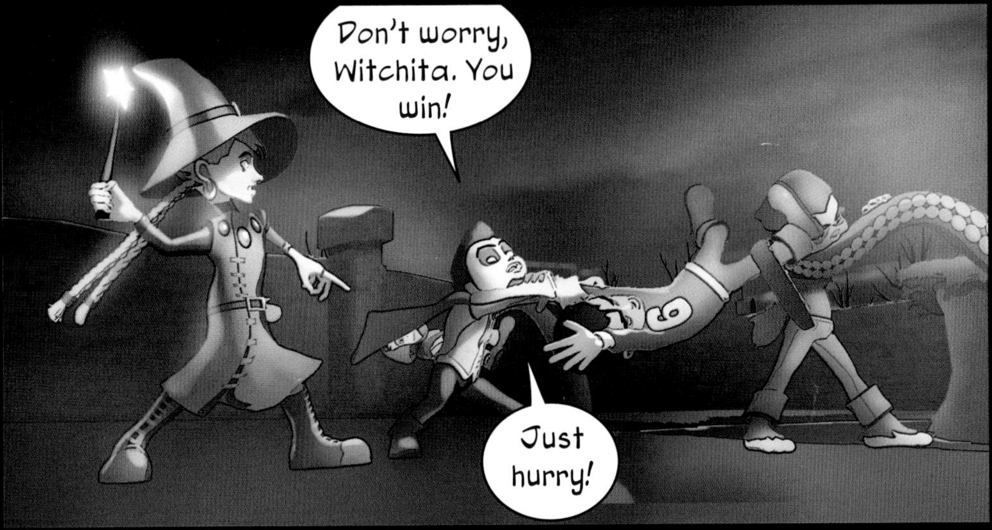
Don't worry, Witchita. You win!
Just hurry!

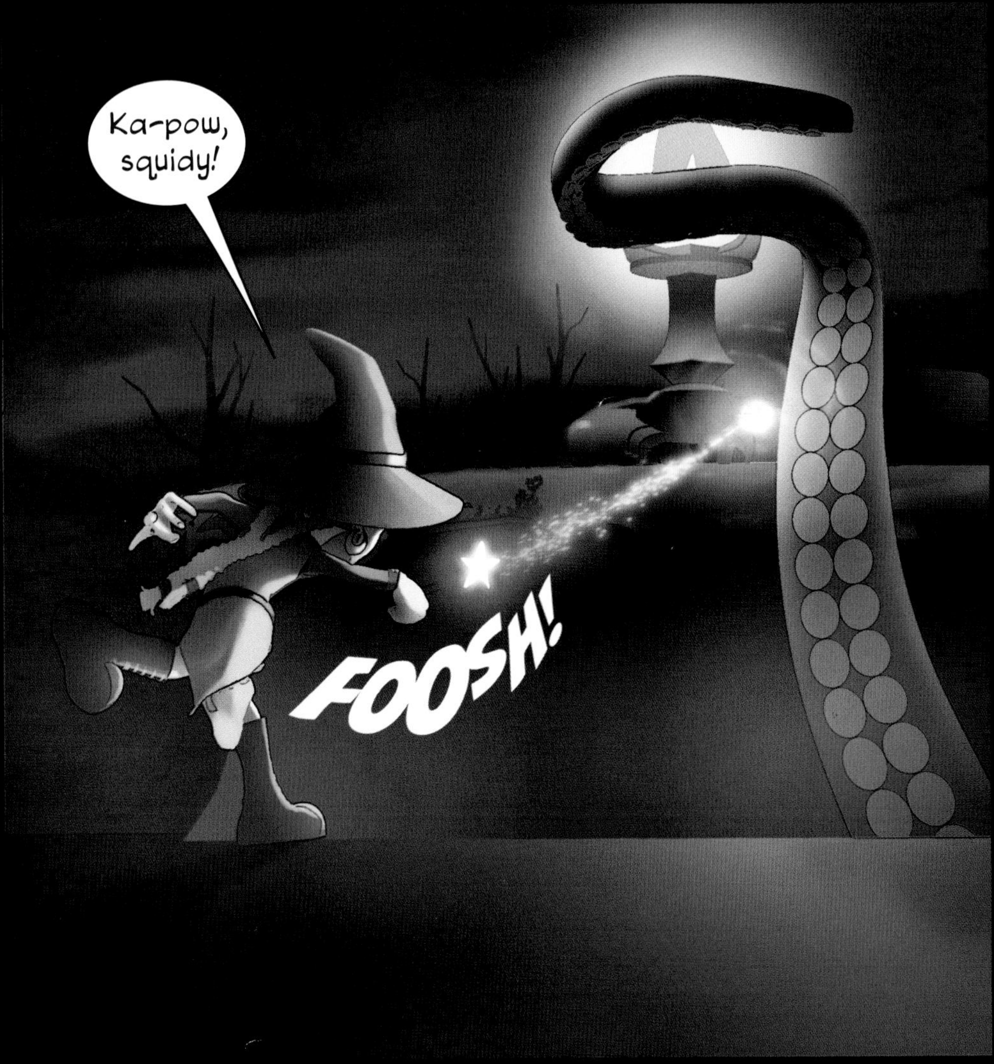
Ka-pow, squidy!
FOOSH!

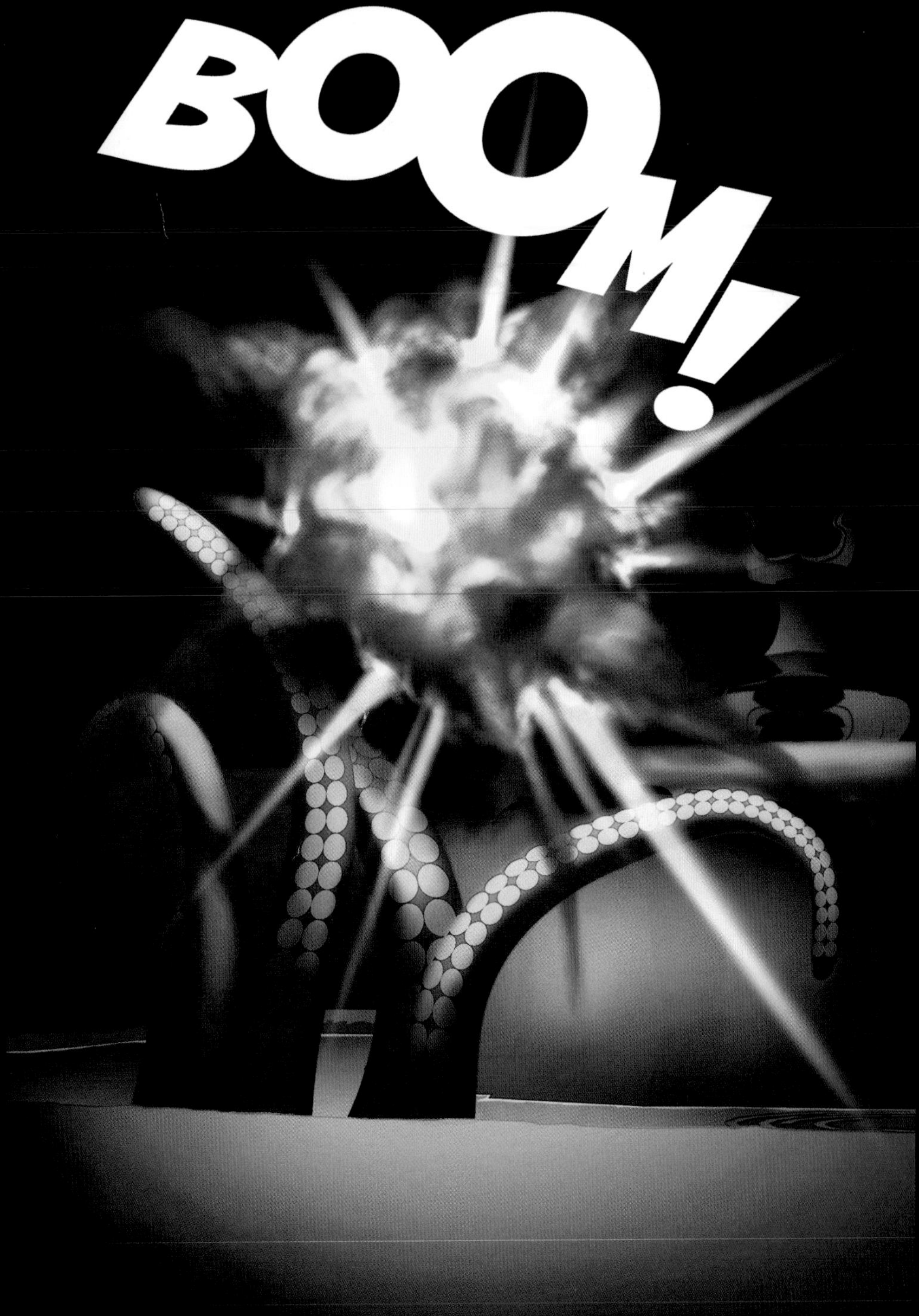
BOOM!

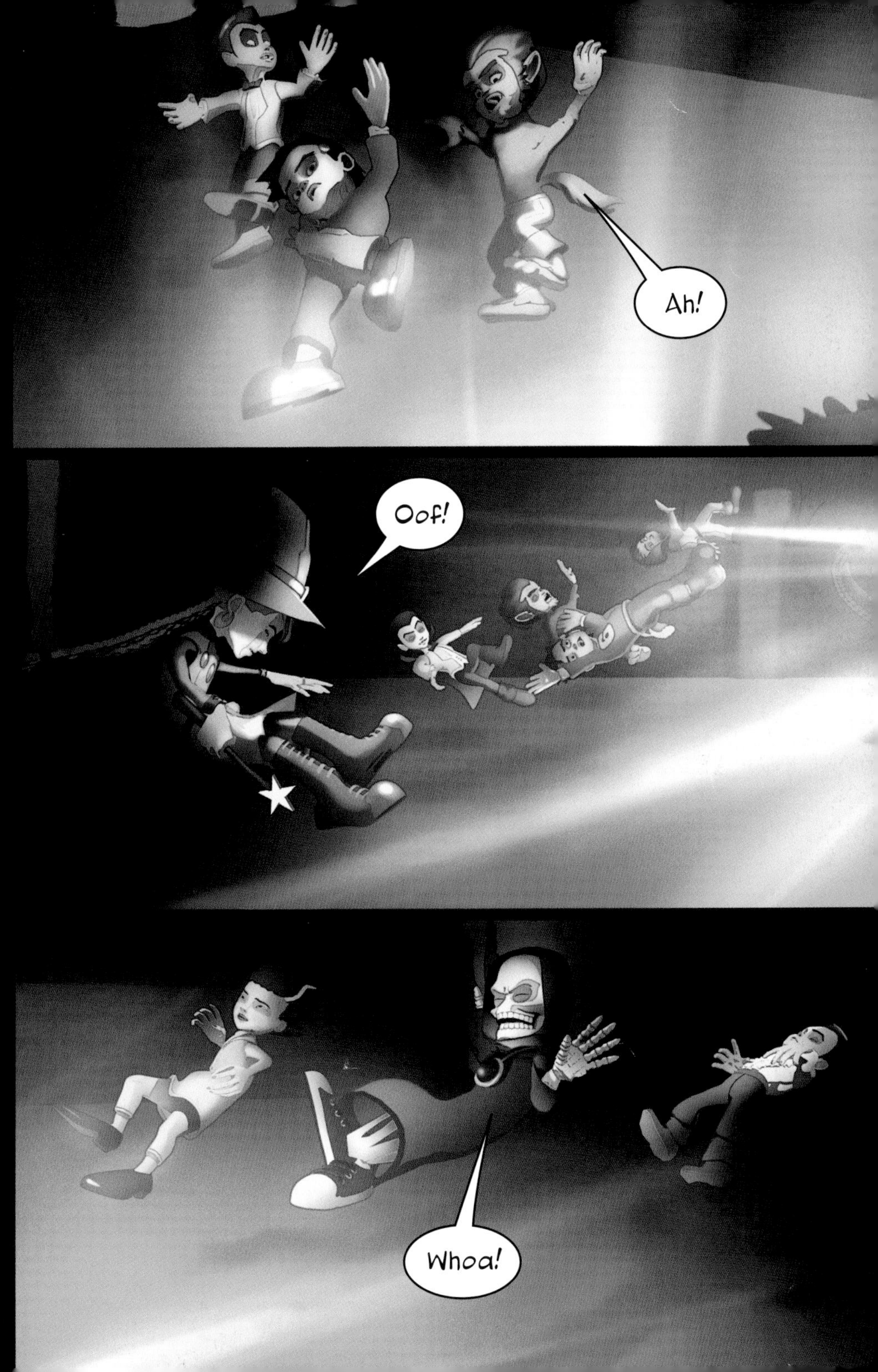
Ah!
Oof!
Whoa!

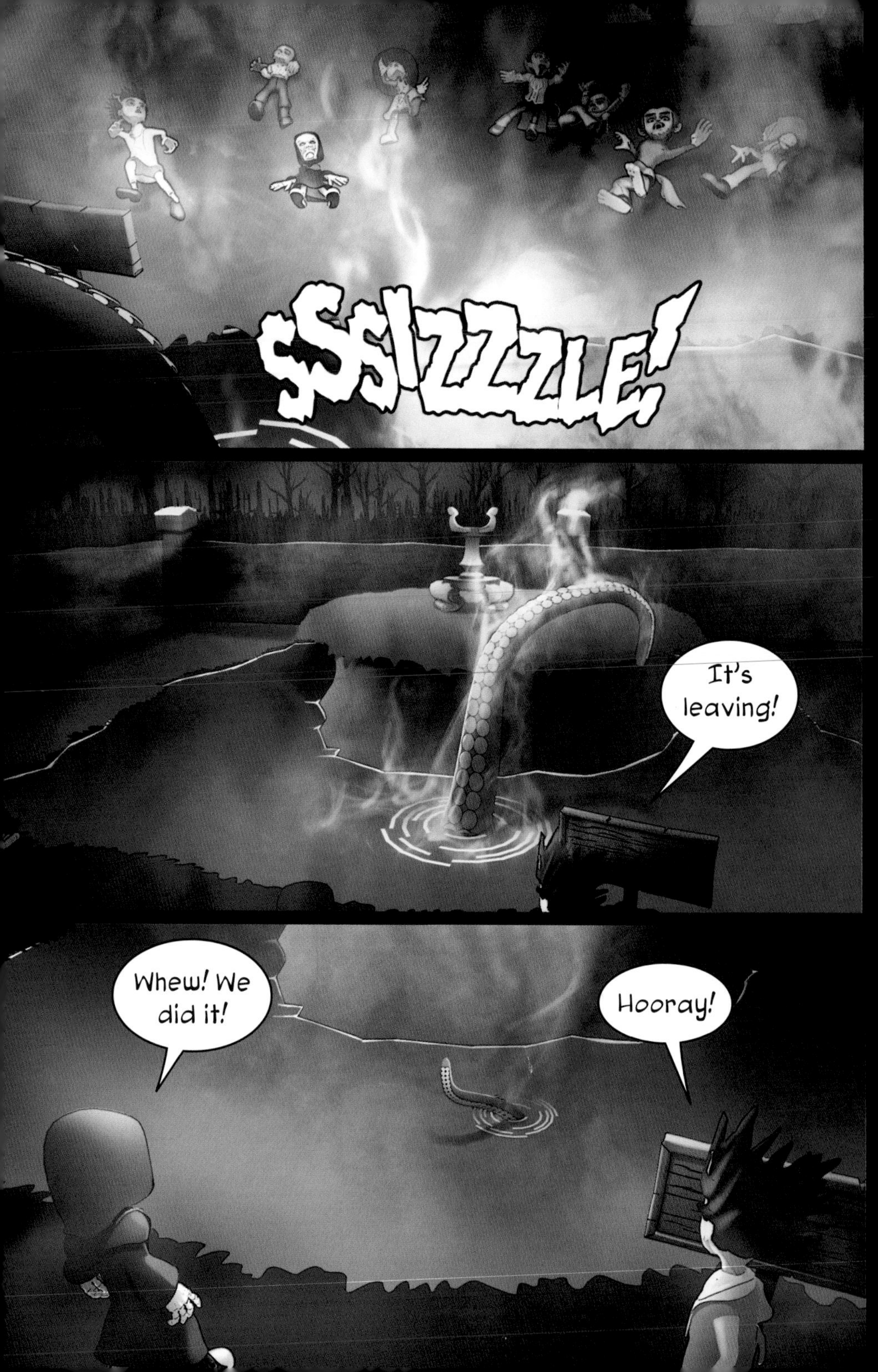
SSIZZZLE!
It's leaving!
Whew! We did it!
Hooray!

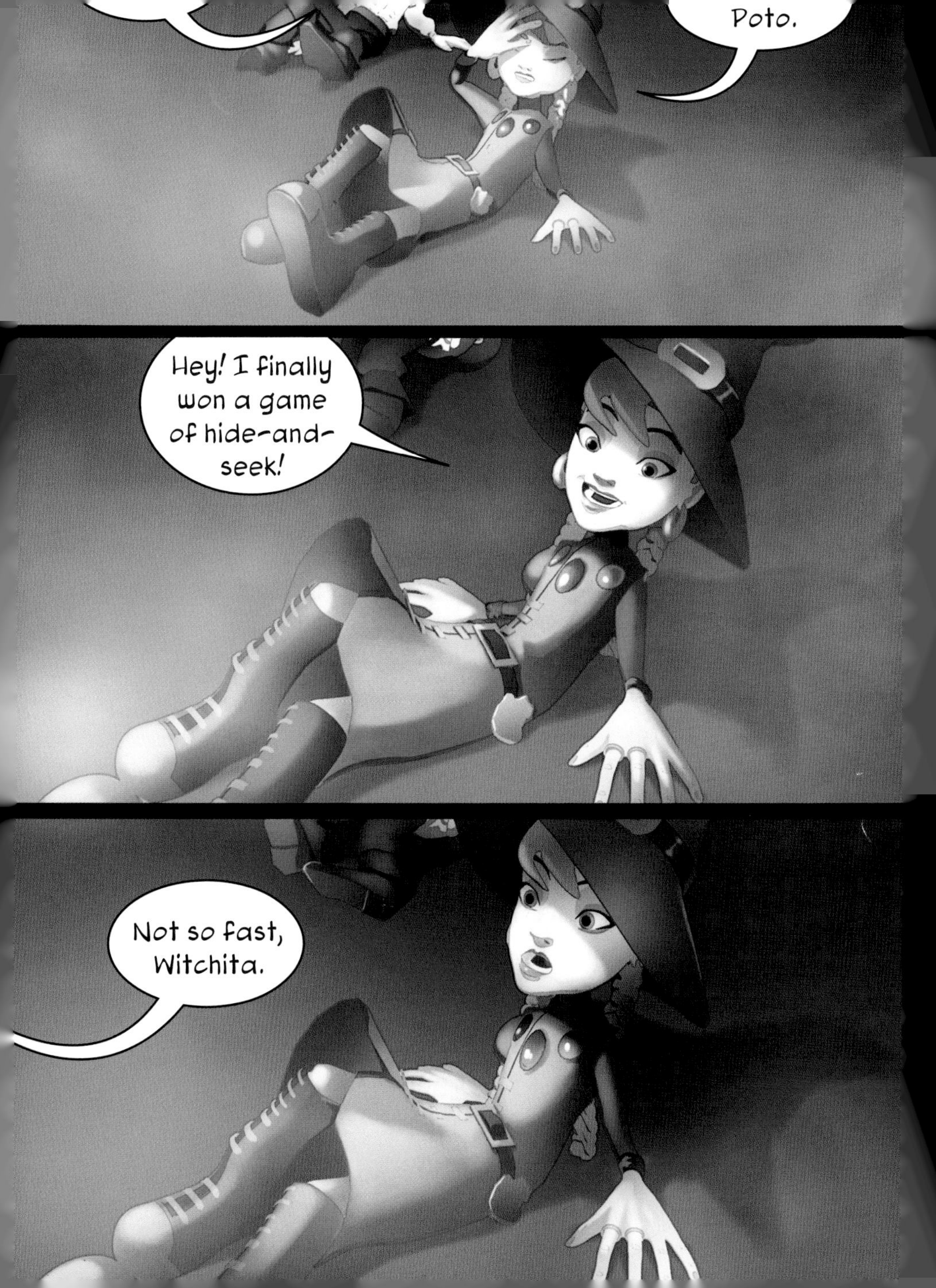
Poto.
Hey! I finally won a game of hide-and-seek!
Not so fast, Witchita.

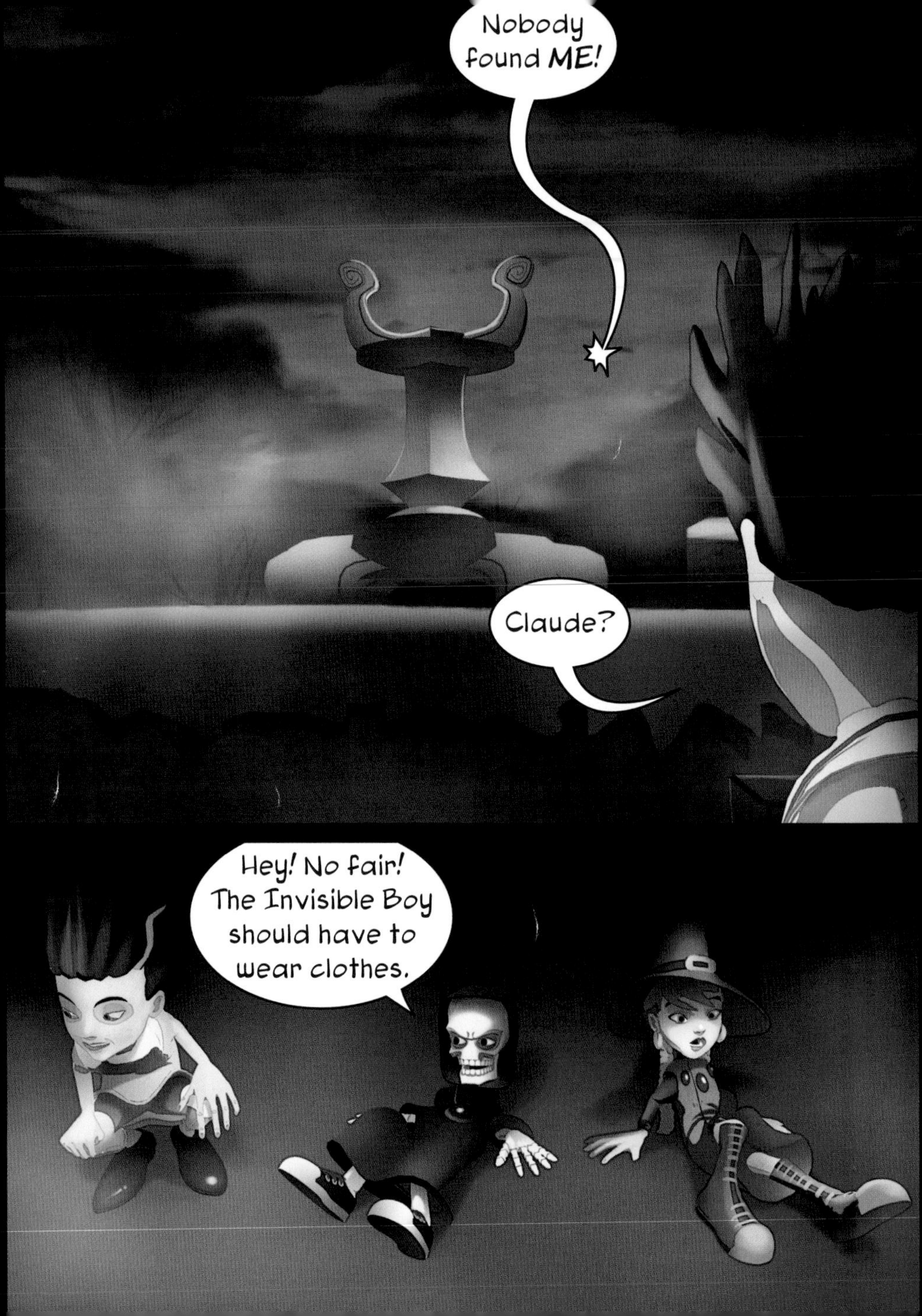
Nobody found **ME!**
Claude?
Hey! No fair! The Invisible Boy should have to wear clothes.

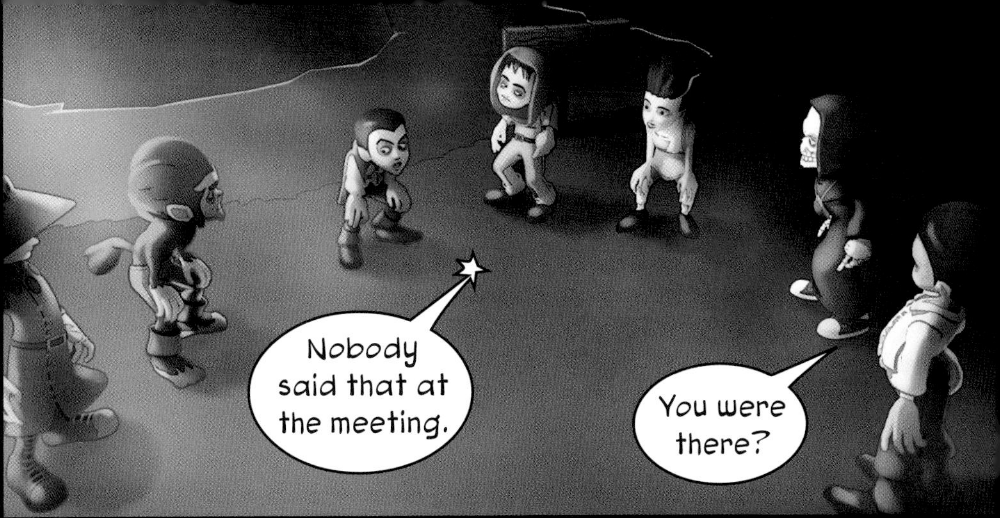
Nobody said that at the meeting.
You were there?

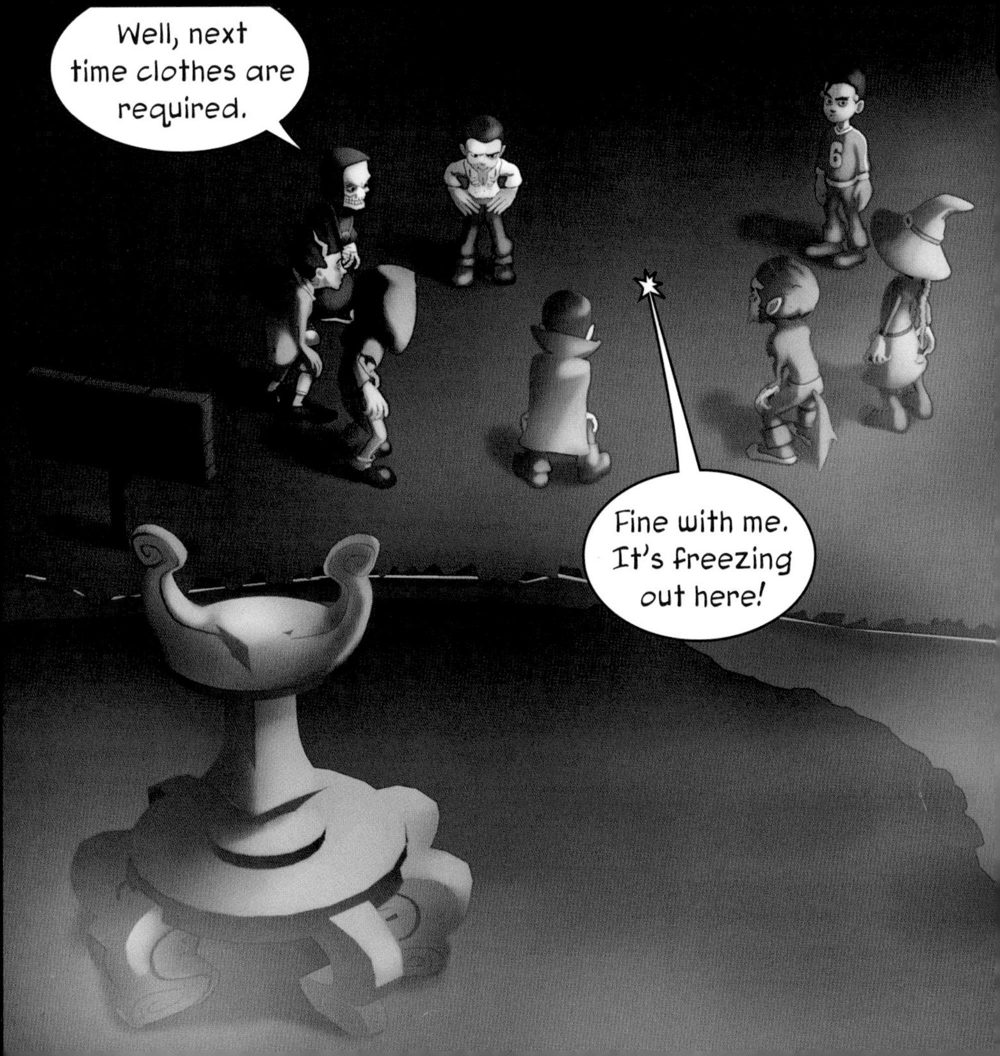
Well, next time clothes are required.
Fine with me. It's freezing out here!

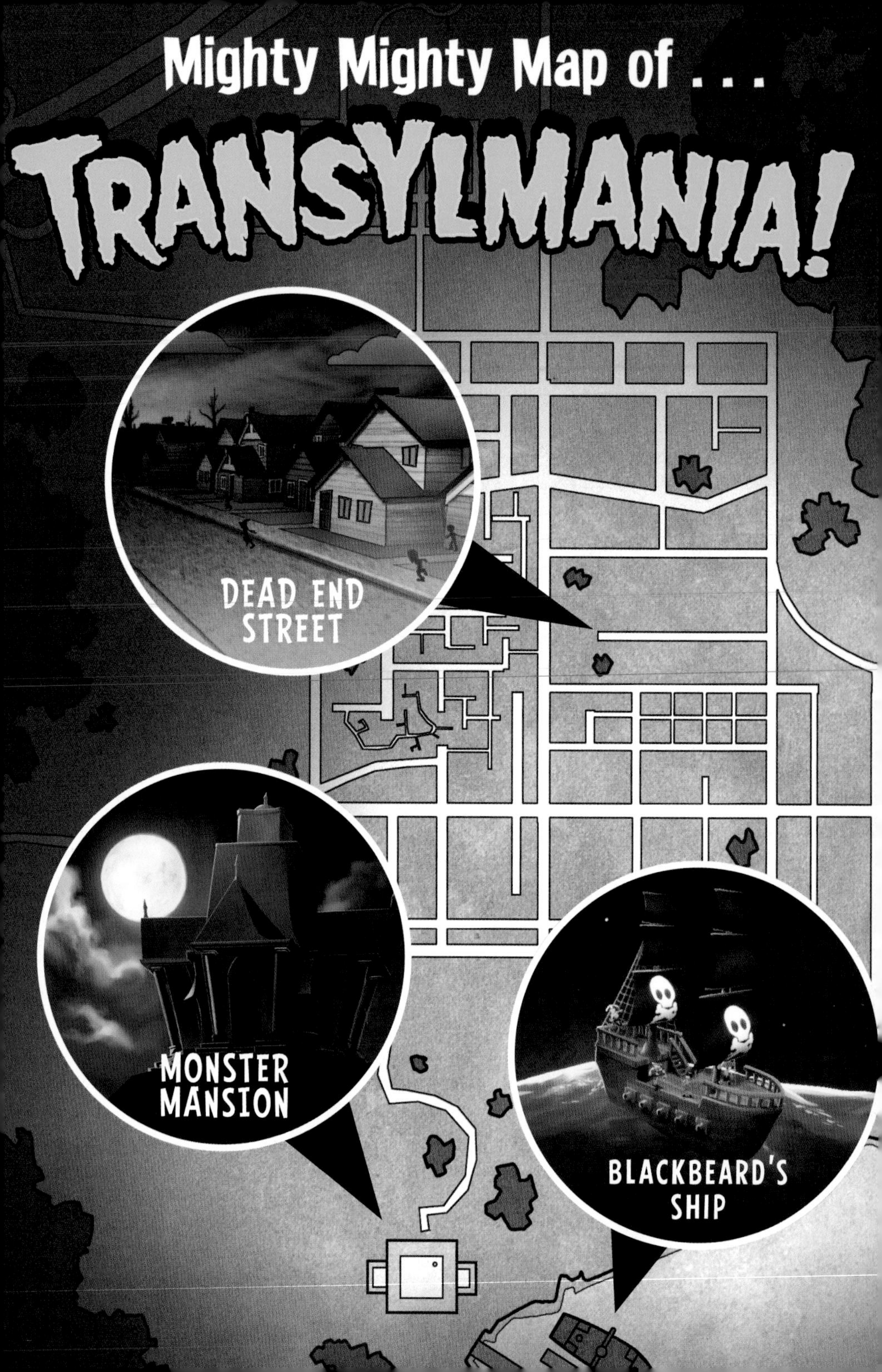
Mighty Mighty Map of . . .
TRANSYLMANIA!
DEAD END STREET
MONSTER MANSION
BLACKBEARD'S SHIP

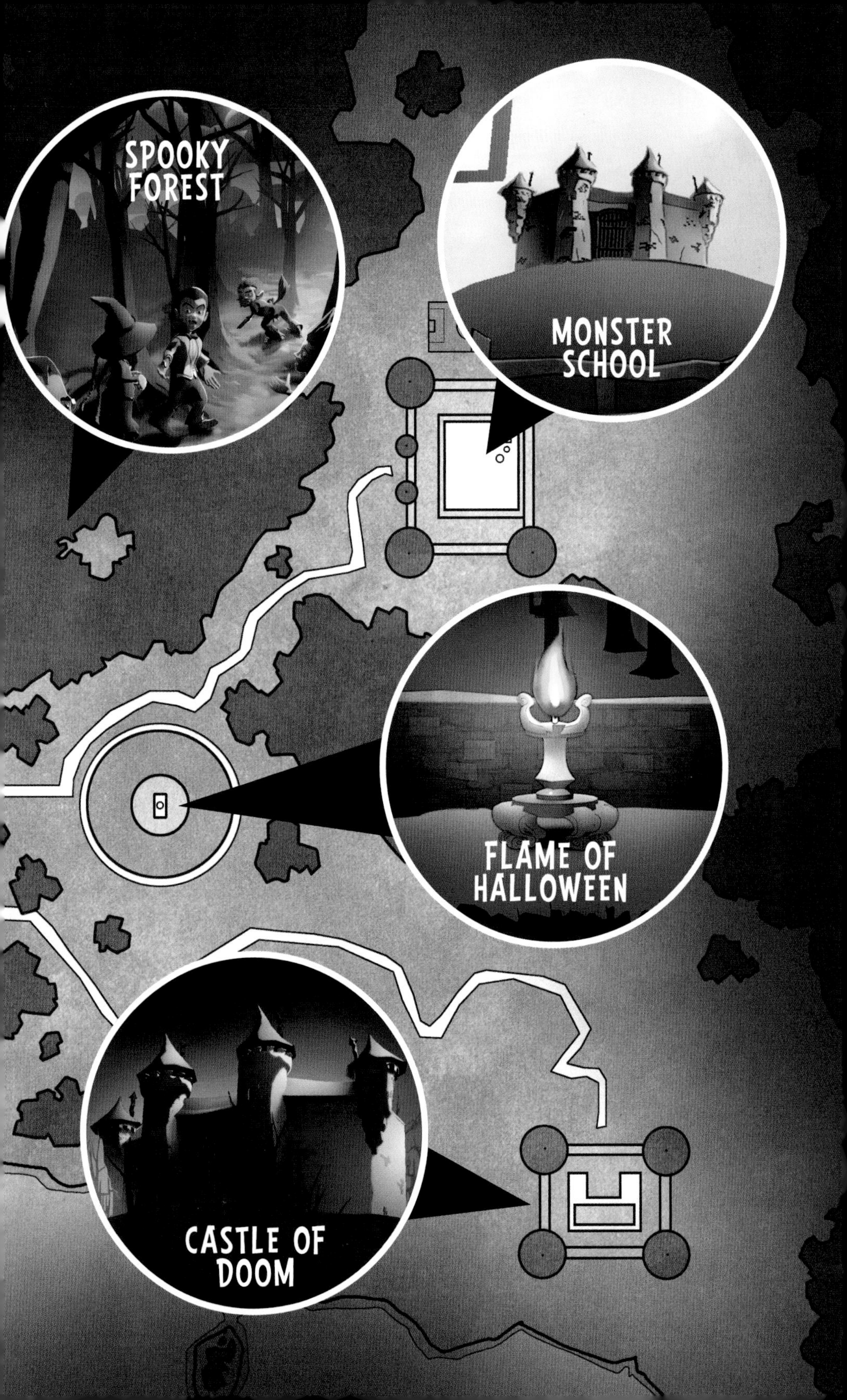
SPOOKY FOREST
MONSTER SCHOOL
FLAME OF HALLOWEEN
CASTLE OF DOOM

Mighty Mighty MONSTERS

...BEFORE THEY WERE STARS!

VLAD

Nickname: The Count

Hometown: Transylmania

Favorite Color: Blood red

Favorite Animal: Bats

Mighty Mighty Powers: the ability to live forever; the power of flight; able to transform into a bat; superpowered fangs.

BIOGRAPHY

Every team needs a leader, and Vlad is more than happy to fill that role for the Mighty Mighty Monsters. Although he's a picky eater (hates garlic, but loves blood!), Vlad never met a monster he didn't like. When a member of the Mighty Mighty Monsters is in trouble, he's always willing to lend a hand (or a wing). These days, Vlad is still one of the most famous monsters on Earth.

WHERE ARE THEY NOW?

In 1897, author Bram Stoker published *Dracula*, the first book ever written about this blood-sucking monster.

Some believe the author based the novel on a real-life person known as Vlad Dracula. In the mid-1400s, this evil leader ruled over what is today Romania.

In 1931, actor Bela Lugosi starred in a movie adaptation of the novel. Since then, this popular film has been selected for preservation in the United States National Film Registry by the Library of Congress.

About Sean O'Reilly
and Arcana Studio

As a lifelong comics fan, Sean O'Reilly dreamed of becoming a comic book creator. In 2004, he realized that dream by creating Arcana Studio. In one short year, O'Reilly took his studio from a one-person operation in his basement to an award-winning comic book publisher with more than 150 graphic novels produced for Harper Collins, Simon & Schuster, Random House, Scholastic, and others.

Within a year, the company won many awards including the Shuster Award for Outstanding Publisher and the Moonbeam Award for top children's graphic novel. O'Reilly also won the Top 40 Under 40 award from the city of Vancouver and authored *The Clockwork Girl* for Top Graphic Novel at Book Expo America in 2009.

Currently, O'Reilly is one of the most prolific independent comic book writers in Canada. While showing no signs of slowing down in comics, he now writes screenplays and adapts his creations for the big screen.

GLOSSARY

clubhouse (KLUHB-houss)—a house used by a group or club

competition (kom-puh-TISH-uhn)—a contest of some kind, such as a game of hide-and-seek

gavel (GAV-uhl)—a small, wooden mallet often used to begin a meeting or to call for quiet

insurance (in-SHU-ruhnss)—protection against sickness, theft, accidents, or losses

Kraken (KRA-kin)—a sea monster

moat (MOHT)—a deep, wide ditch filled with water, which surrounds a building or area to protect it

mood (MOOD)—the way a person feels

motion (MOH-shuhn)—a formal suggestion made at a meeting

Mozart (MOTE-sart)—a famous composer of music who lived during the 1700s

provide (pruh-VIDE)—to supply the things that someone needs

required (ri-KWIRED)—something that must be done

DISCUSSION QUESTIONS

1. What Mighty Mighty Monster do you think would be the most difficult to find in a game of hide-and-seek? Why?

2. Witchita had to break the rules of the game to save her friend. Do you think this decision was okay? Explain.

3. All of the Mighty Mighty Monsters are different. Which character do you like the best and why?

WRITING PROMPTS

1. In this story, the Mighty Mighty Monsters make up their own rules for hide-and-seek. Write down the rules for your very own game. Give it a name. Then see if others want to play!

2. If you could be any monster, which monster would you be? Write about your choice and the adventures you would have.

3. Write your own Mighty Mighty Monsters adventure. What will the ghoulish gang do next? What villains will they face? You decide.

Mighty Mighty MONSTERS ADVENTURES

Mighty Mighty MONSTERS
The KING of HALLOWEEN CASTLE
GRAPHIC NOVEL
by Sean O'Reilly

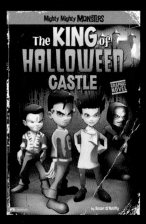

The King of Halloween Castle

Mighty Mighty MONSTERS
NEW MONSTER in SCHOOL
GRAPHIC NOVEL
by Sean O'Reilly

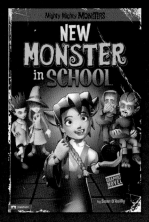

New Monster in School

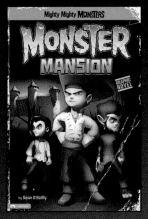

Mighty Mighty MONSTERS
MONSTER MANSION
GRAPHIC NOVEL
by Sean O'Reilly

Monster Mansion

Mighty Mighty MONSTERS
My MISSING MONSTER
by Sean O'Reilly
GRAPHIC NOVEL

My Missing Monster

Mighty Mighty MONSTERS
Lost in SPOOKY FOREST
by Sean O'Reilly
GRAPHIC NOVEL

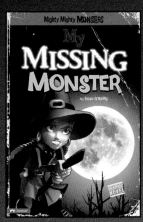

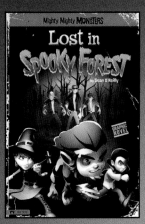

Lost in Spooky Forest